FRA

When a Boss Steals Your Heart 2

Kat Washington

When a Boss Steals Your Heart 2

Copyright © 2016 by Kat Washington

Table of Contents

Chapter One

Los

None of this shit felt real. I felt like I was just having a nightmare, and I would soon wake up from it with Alani lying beside me. That's what I was waiting for. I was waiting for Alani to walk through the front door with bags from every store in the mall in her hands. I was waiting for her to kiss me all over my face to wake me up and ask what I wanted for breakfast. I was especially waiting for her to call me and let me know that she was just playing a sick prank on me and she would be home soon. But I knew that none of that was going to happen. I would be waiting forever for her to come back to me.

This wasn't supposed to happen. She wasn't just supposed to leave me like this. She wasn't supposed to find out about C.J like she did either. All of this was my fault. Now I've lost the best thing that's ever happened to me because I couldn't man up and tell her what was up. I didn't cheat on Alani when Tammy got pregnant. Now that I think about it, Alani probably wouldn't have even been mad once I told her the full story. I was wishing that Alani and I could trade places right now. She didn't deserve any of this that happened.

When the doctor came out and told us that Alani was dead, I didn't know what to do. I wanted to fight the doctor even though it wasn't even his fault. To be honest, I wanted to die too. I just wanted to be wherever Alani was. Life had no purpose without her. I didn't even go home. I just sat in the waiting room for hours. I've never cried so hard before in my life. Langston had to come back and get my ass because I didn't plan on leaving at all.

The funeral was a blur. I made sure to pay for everything because I wanted my baby to go out in style. Jaxon wanted to help because she was his only sister, but I wasn't having that. All of this was my fault anyway, so it was only right that I did this. There wasn't a lot of people that came to the funeral, but that was expected. All that mattered was the people who cared about her was there.

I stood in the cemetery after everyone had left. Even though she was so messed up from the crash that she couldn't have an open casket, it was still a beautiful ceremony. A couple of tears fell from my eyes as I stood over her grave. We didn't even get to have a wedding like I had planned. There was so much that I wanted to do but I couldn't, because now she was gone forever. No one could get in contact with Lena so she wasn't even at the funeral.

"You okay?" I heard from behind me. I turned around and seen Londyn standing there. What the hell was she even doing here? How the hell did she know that I would be here?

"Yeah, I'm good." I said wiping my face.

"She's in a better place now. Everything happens for a reason. It will get easier to deal with as the days go on." she told me. I didn't even say anything back. I know that Alani would not want her here. I shouldn't even be entertaining her ass right now.

"I gotta go. I'll see you later." I said walking off. It was a nice, sunny day, but I felt like shit on the inside. I couldn't even go home, so I just decided to go to my mom's house and stay over there until I got myself together.

Pulling up to her house, I slowly got out of my car and walked up to the door. Right now, I just wanted to sleep until the pain I was feeling went away. I don't think this pain would ever go away though. I was going to have to deal with this for the rest of my life. I probably won't ever find a girl that I loved like I loved Alani.

"Hey Carlos, how are you feeling?" my mom asked. I didn't even say anything to her. I just walked straight upstairs and collapsed on the bed. I just wanted to be left alone for the next two weeks. Shit, or two months.

"Carlos!" Alani yelled. She was standing in our bedroom in a beautiful white dress. Her skin was glowing, and her hair was actually straight and flowing down her back. She looked like an angel. My angel.

"Carlos, wake up! You have to come save me!" she yelled.

"Save you from where?" I asked inching towards her.

"Helpppppppp meeeeeee!" she screamed. She had tears streaming down her face, and all I wanted to do was hug her so I could stop the pain that she was feeling. I reached out for her but she disappeared. The bedroom turned into the road that she got into that car wreck on. I was standing in the grass watching the whole thing happen. When she flew out

of the windshield, I ran over to her to see if she was okay. She was all bruised up and had cuts all over her face. She looked lifeless lying there.

"Alani." I whispered. Her eyes flew open, and she gave me the coldest stare ever.

"This is all your fault." she said, before she lifted a gun and shot me in the face.

I sat straight up in bed and looked around. It was pitch black in the room, and I noticed that I wasn't in my bed. That's when I remembered that I was at my mom's place. I shook my head and got out of the bed to go downstairs. I had been having the same dream for a couple of days now. I didn't know what it meant, but I knew it always made me feel worse than I already did.

My mom was sitting at the kitchen table when I got downstairs. She had a worried look on her face, and I didn't like it one bit.

"What are you still doing up?" I asked her.

"Son, I'm worried about you." she said drinking her tea.

"Why? I'm fine." I lied. She gave me a knowing look. She knew damn well I was lying.

"You're far from fine. I can see it all in your eyes, and I heard you screaming for Alani in your sleep." I didn't even know that I was yelling in my sleep. I needed to get it together.

"I know you're going through it right now, but it will get better. I don't need you doing anything crazy because

4

Alani is gone. I know you feel incomplete without here, but allow yourself to heal. Don't start doing things without thinking it through first." I didn't understand why she was telling me this. I wasn't even doing anything.

"I'm not going to do anything, Ma." I assured her. I kissed her on her cheek and went back upstairs to try and get some rest.

Two weeks later

Everything still felt the same. I still felt incomplete without Alani, and I still have the same dream every night. It's getting to a point where I don't even want to sleep anymore. I started popping pills just because I needed something stronger than weed to help me feel numb. Weed just wasn't doing the trick.

I woke up on the couch from sleep that I didn't even mean to have. I checked my phone to see if I had any missed calls. I had a couple of text messages from Londyn, Langston, and Ali. I didn't care about nothing Ali and Lang was talking about right now, but I decided to see what Londyn wanted.

Londyn: Just checking on u. Maybe you should stop by just to let me know ur good

I read the text message and thought why not? I didn't have anything better to do. I sat up on the couch and looked at the coffee table. There were two pills on the table that I meant to take before I fell asleep. I put them both in my mouth and swallowed them with the Ciroc that was sitting on the table. The alcohol burned my throat a little bit, but I didn't care. I got off of the couch, grabbed my car keys, and was out of the door, heading to my car.

I had bought me a small condo to stay at, but I couldn't stay in that big ass estate anymore. All I did was think about Alani, and it had me ready to go crazy. There were just too many memories in that damn house. I was thinking about selling it and just finding me a new house altogether.

By the time I got to Londyn's crib, I could feel the effects of the pills starting to kick in. I felt like I was floating on a cloud, and I was feeling good as hell. I walked up to Londyn's door and knocked on it.

When she opened the door and looked at me and said, "Hey, you should've told me that you were on your way." she smiled at me.

"I do what I want." I told her stepping into the house. Londyn had on a black wig that came past her shoulders. She looked like she was starting to gain a little bit of weight back too. I was happy for her. I didn't want her to lose her life to cancer. I wouldn't even want my worst enemy to lose their life to cancer. That's just a fucked up situation.

"What brings you by?" she asked, as I sat down on the couch and turned on the T.V.

"I was bored, so I came over here. You got anything to drink?"

"Like water?"

"Do I look like I want some damn water? Do you have any liquor?" I snapped at her. She looked shocked at how I had talked to her but I didn't care. These pills were turning me into a rude ass nigga, but I didn't care about that either. They made me forget the pain I was feeling so I was going to keep fucking with them.

Londyn got up and went to the kitchen. She came back with a big bottle of Paul Masson and a couple of shot glasses. She handed me the bottle and the shot glass. What the fuck was I gonna do with that? I put the shot glass on the table then opened the bottle. I took it straight to the head, and she was just staring at me with wide eyes.

"What the fuck you looking at me like that for? You never seen a nigga drink before?" I asked.

"Los, are you sure you're okay?" she asked with a concerned look.

"Yeah, I'm fine. Get the fuck out my business." I shot back. She didn't say anything back. She took the bottle from me and poured her own shot. She shook her head at me.

"You're changing. And it's not for the better." she said sadly.

"Yeah, whatever. Go make a nigga something to eat. I haven't ate shit and I'm starving." I said flipping through the channels again. She stared at me for a minute before she finally got her ass up and went into the kitchen. I searched my pockets for another pill but I couldn't find one. I guess I had left all of them at home. Now I didn't even want to be here anymore.

By the time Londyn had finished cooking, I was drunk as hell. I had finished off half of the bottle by my damn self. Londyn came back into the living room and put a plate in my lap. It was steak with mashed potatoes and gravy and some green beans. This shit looked and smelled good as hell and I dug right in. I had to admit, Londyn did her thing in the kitchen, and I was tired as hell when I finished eating. I sat the plate on the coffee table, and I made my way upstairs. I took my clothes off as I made my way to her bedroom. I just wanted to sleep. If she had a problem with me sleeping in her bed, then oh well. I really didn't give a fuck about how she was feeling. Fuck everyone's feelings.

I woke up the next morning with Londyn laying on my chest. She didn't have her wig on, and she wasn't looking as good as she did the night before. I gently pushed her off of me and sat up. I had a banging ass headache, and my mouth felt dry as shit. I got up to go relieve my bladder, then I started putting my clothes back on.

"Where are you rushing off to?" Londyn asked.

"None of your damn business."

"Okay, I just asked you a damn question. You don't have to be so damn rude." She sat up in bed and folded her arms.

"Stop asking me questions then." I said, then walked out of the house. I didn't have a reason to be acting like that towards Londyn, but she wasn't my bitch. I might hit her up later, but until then, there was business that needed to be handled.

Chapter Two

Londyn

My plan was working out perfectly. Alani was out of the picture, and I was working on getting close to Los again. I wasn't feeling how rude he was acting towards me, but at least I got him to come over. Then he even slept in my bed. If I wanted to, I could've had sex with him, because he was sloppy drunk, but I decided not to.

The day that Alani got into that car wreck, Jasmine and I were the ones who cut her brake lines, and I even removed the screws from her front tire. That's how she lost control of her car. It was even better that it started pouring down with rain.

My cousin worked at the hospital that she was brought into. I got my cousin to tell them that she died so that Darius, Jasmine and I could get her body and move it to the basement of Darius' house. At first, my cousin wasn't feeling the idea of him telling Los that she was dead, but as soon as I threatened to tell his wife about all the women he had be cheating with, he quickly got on board.

I walked into Darius' house and seen him sitting on the couch watching T.V. He was on drugs really bad now because of me. The only difference is, I quit and he couldn't. I didn't know where Jasmine was. She had been acting different ever since I made her lose her baby. I still didn't care though. She shouldn't have tried to beat my ass. Maybe she could still be pregnant, but oh well. That's her fault.

Darius looked at me and smiled when he saw me walk through the door. He wasn't as good looking as he was when I first saw him. He was way too skinny now, and I wasn't feeling that. Plus, I had my bae Carlos back in my life, so I didn't even need to fuck him anymore.

"You looking good enough to eat." he said, licking his crusty ass lips. I rolled my eyes; I know I was looking good. I was eating like a fat bitch so that I could gain my weight back, and I was also growing my hair back. I didn't have to lie about having brain cancer anymore, but I was still wearing wigs though, because I looked crazy as hell. Soon enough, I would have enough hair that I can actually style.

"I know." I said to him. He stood up but I kept on walking towards the basement. I had to see how this bitch was doing. I guess I could've just killed her ass, but I felt like that was too easy. I wanted her to know that I was with Los, and I was going to hold her hostage forever. I smiled just thinking about how hurt she's going to be when it's me living in the big ass house, wearing the wedding ring, and having all of his babies, and I couldn't wait.

We had turned the basement into a little hospital room so that Alani could heal properly, because she had a few broken ribs and some really bad bruises all over her body. It was Darius' idea to do this, because I honestly didn't care if the bitch healed properly or not.

When I walked in the basement, she was sleeping. That's all her ass did now. I mean, there wasn't nothing else she could really do. She couldn't move around, and she couldn't get out the basement. I wanted to hit her in the face as she slept, and I couldn't believe Los had left me for her. I guess she felt me looking at her because her eyes shot open.

"Please let me go home." she said, barely above a whisper.

"Bitch, shut the fuck up. This is your new home now, so you need to get used to it." I spat.

"Does Carlos know you're doing this?"

"Carlos doesn't give a fuck about you! He has a child, and he's ready to start a family with me, so we had to find a way to get rid of you. You were supposed to die in that car crash, but since you didn't, he told me to get rid of you." I smiled at her. She didn't say anything else. She just let the tears fall, and she turned her back towards me. I chuckled and left out of the room. I needed to make her think that Carlos didn't want her anymore. It looked like I was doing a pretty good job at it too.

"I'll be back later. I got some shit I need to handle." I told Darius and walked out of the house. Tammy thought everything was good between us, but she was dead wrong. She really thinks she can have a baby by my man and get away

13

with it? Hell no. She has to die, and I'm going to be playing step mommy to that little baby.

Pulling up to Tammy's house, I got pissed off all over again. This bitch really fucked my man behind my back! I can't trust any of these bitches, I swear. I turned my car off and just sat there for a while thinking about how I wanted to kill her with my bare hands. I wasn't going to do that though. I had to make this quick and easy.

I jumped out of my car and walked up to her front door. I was just going to knock and wait for her to open the door, but I had something else in mind. I walked around to the back of her house and found a big ass rock. I threw it at the glass door and the whole thing shattered, then I smiled as I stepped into the house.

"Hello? Is someone there?" I heard Tammy say. I didn't understand why people did that. Why call out to the person that's trying to kill you? If anything, shut your ass up and try to hide. Make the killer think you're not home or some shit. I shook my head and pulled my pistol out.

"Hello?" she called again. She walked down the stairs and came into the living room where I was standing.

"Londyn? What are you doing here? What the hell happened to the back door?!" she yelled. She didn't see that I had a gun in my hand, and I could tell that she was obviously upset.

"Hi, Tammy." I smiled.

"Did you do this? Why didn't you just ring the doorbell or some shit?" I laughed at her.

"That would've been too easy, love. And I didn't want to wake the baby."

"You still could've rang the doorbell. You're paying to get this fixed. I am not sleeping here with my damn back door like this." she fussed.

"Oh, you won't even have to worry about doors where you're going."

"What? What do you mean?" She was so clueless. I raised my gun and aimed it at her head. Her eyes widened, and I could see the fear written all over her face.

"W-What are you doing with that?" she stuttered.

"Did you really think you were going to fuck my man, have a baby by him, and think I was just going to let you live?"

"It wasn't supposed to happen, it was a mistake!" she cried. Tears were streaming down her face, but I wasn't moved by them at all.

"You knew I loved him! I vented to you about him all the time and you go and do this shit? Then you expected me to just be okay with it?" I yelled getting even angrier.

"You loved him, but he doesn't love you! He loved Alani, and he always will. I don't want him. I just had to see what all the fuss was about since you were always bragging about his big ass dick. Now you're in here with a gun in my face, and he still doesn't want you. He just lost the girl he loves. What makes you think he'll love you now?" she asked. I didn't like how she was talking to me like I didn't have a gun in her face.

"Bitch, fuck you! Alani is not dead. I kidnapped her ass so that Carlos could finally see what he had with me."

"Londyn, you're fucking crazy. Please don't kill me. I have a son to live for now." She cried some more. Her pleas fell on deaf ears though. I shot her twice sending two bullets right in her skull. She fell to the floor hard as hell, and I smiled as I looked at her dead body. Now she'd learned her lesson. You don't go around fucking other people's man. Then the bitch was supposed to be my friend and all that.

I hurried out of her house the same way that I came in. I didn't want her nosey neighbors to see me and call the police or some shit. I jumped in my car and sped out of her neighborhood. I felt so much better knowing that I killed that bitch. I already knew that Carlos was going to need a shoulder to cry on, and I was going to be right there when he found out that Tammy's hoe ass was dead. I couldn't stop myself from smiling even if I wanted to. My plan was working out perfectly. Carlos would be asking to marry me in no time, and I couldn't wait.

Chapter Three

Alani

I didn't know how to feel right now. I knew Londyn's ass was crazy, but I didn't know if she was telling the truth. Did Carlos really let her do this shit to me just so he could be with her crazy ass? Did he know that I was locked in this damn basement, and she wasn't feeding me at all? I couldn't do anything but lay there and cry. I was so heartbroken, and it was tearing me up because after the crash, I couldn't remember shit. I remember seeing that Carlos had a whole family though. Right under my nose. He looked so shocked to see me when I approached them, and it was still blowing my mind that he hid all of this from me. You can't trust anybody these days, not even the nigga you're sleeping with.

I should've just stayed away from him and Darius. Men are no good and all they do is cause heartaches and pain. I always give my all to a nigga, and I always end up getting shitted on. What the hell? Was it me? Was I not a good enough girlfriend? My pussy obviously had to be whack since I couldn't find a nigga that didn't want to cheat on me. The tears were falling so fast, I couldn't catch them even if I wanted to.

The basement door opened and a woman walked in. I figured it was Londyn, so I didn't look at her at all.

"Here you go. You need to eat something." a familiar voice said. I looked up to see that it was Jasmine, and she was handing me a plate of food and a glass of water.

"Jasmine? You're in on her kidnapping me?" I said, instantly getting pissed off. I didn't want Darius anymore, so I didn't understand why the hell she played a part in this.

"It's a long story that I'll have to tell you later. I know you haven't eaten in a couple of days, so I made you some baked spaghetti." I looked at the food then back up at her.

"I'd rather starve than eat your food." I spat. I didn't like Jasmine, and Jasmine didn't like me. I didn't know why the hell she was trying so hard to be nice to me. She probably poisoned the food, and she was trying to kill me. She actually looked shocked at what I said to her.

"I haven't done anything to the food. Do you want me to eat some first?" I rolled my eyes. I didn't want anything from this bitch, but by the way my stomach was growling, I might eat anything right about now. She sat the plate on the bed then she left me in the basement alone.

I immediately dug in. It felt like I hadn't eaten anything in years, and I wanted more, but I had no way to tell Jasmine. I didn't understand why I was in this basement though. There was no way out whatsoever. I couldn't really get up to walk around either because my body was still sore from the car crash. I still couldn't believe that all this had happened. As soon as I get out of here, I'm killing Londyn, then leaving Miami.

The door opened again and in walked Darius. *Are you fucking serious? Did they really team up just to get rid of me? You've got to be kidding me.* I thought to myself. Darius didn't look like himself at all. He was really skinny, and his face was sunken in. It looked like he hadn't slept in days, and his dreads were a damn mess.

"Hey, Alani. Long time no see." he smiled showing his yellow ass teeth. I couldn't believe that this is the man I used to be so in love with. At one point, I actually did want to have his kids. I'm glad that I didn't though; this nigga looked like he was doing drugs.

"Leave me alone." I said. He smiled at me and kept walking towards me.

"You still look good as hell. I bet that pussy still good too, even though you've been giving it up to that bitch nigga Carlos." I rolled my eyes when he said Carlos' name. Fuck that nigga. His ass couldn't just break up with me like a normal ass person. He really had to go to these great lengths to get rid of me. All he had to do was tell me that he didn't want to be with me anymore, but instead, he wanted to pull this bitch move.

Darius started trying to spread my legs, but I kicked him in his face. I still had on this hospital gown, and I didn't have on any underwear.

"Stop moving, bitch. Let me get some of this good shit." he demanded.

"Fuck you, nigga! Get your dirty ass hands off of me!"
I yelled. I guess I said the wrong thing because he punched
me hard as fuck. My nose started bleeding, and it felt like he
had broken it, but I wasn't sure. I wanted to cry from the
pain, but I didn't want him to think he was breaking me
down. I bit my lip and chuckled.

"That's all you got? You hit like a pussy." I said, wiping
my nose with the back of my hand.

"Shut the fuck up, bitch!" he roared. I just laughed at
him because he was mad. He slapped me hard as hell and
made me bite my tongue. Blood filled my mouth, and I
wanted to throw up.

"You ain't talking that big shit no more, huh?" he
asked with a smirk on his face. I spat blood all over his face,
and I swear I seen this nigga's eyes turn black. He started
raining blows all over my body. This was even more painful
because my body was already sore. He was beating me like I
had stolen something from him. I couldn't do anything but lay
there and take it. I know my eye was swollen because I could
barely see out of it. When he was finished, he spat on me and
slapped me one more time.

"I'll be back later to get some of that good as pussy."
he smiled and left the basement. As soon as he left, I broke
down crying. It wasn't one of those suffer in silence type of
cries either. I was sobbing loud as hell. I had never gotten my
ass beat like that. Especially by Darius. I wanted to get up and

go to the bathroom but I couldn't move. My body was in so much pain. I just laid there and ended up drifting off to sleep.

I woke up to cold ass water and ice being thrown on me. I sat straight up but quickly laid back down because of the shooting pain that shot through my ribs.

"Damn bitch, you look terrible." Londyn said laughing. I wanted to kill her. Just looking up at her face made my blood boil. I needed to find a way to get out of here. Londyn was going to die.

"Fuck you." I said to her.

"Oh, don't worry. Los and I will be doing plenty of that later on tonight. I might even tell him not to pull out this time. I think it's time for us to start a family." she smiled. I wanted to cry, but I didn't. I just rolled my eyes at her ass. I couldn't wait until I was able to kill her.

"I'll be back later to tell you all about our evening. I might even record it so that you can watch it on the big screen." She blew me a kiss and walked out of the basement. The way I was feeling right now, I might end up killing Carlos too. I had enough of people treating me like shit. I'm nice to everybody, and this is what I get in return? Oh hell no. People really had me fucked up.

I didn't even know that I had fallen asleep until I felt my legs being pulled apart. My eyes shot right open, and Darius was naked as the day he was born. I could see his ribs. His body used to be the shit, but now it wasn't shit at all. He climbed on top of me, and I tried my hardest to fight him but my body was weak, and he was strong as hell.

"Stop fucking moving!" he yelled punching me in the face. After that, I just laid there and let him do whatever he wanted to do to me. Without warning, he shoved his entire dick inside of me. That was one thing that was still the same about him. It was still thick and long, but I was dry as hell and it hurt like hell. Tears fell from my eyes as he pumped in and out of me. I had never felt any pain like this. He grabbed my face and tried to kiss me but I turned my head. That's when he slapped the shit out of me then tried again.

His breath smelled like pure shit. Like he hadn't brushed his teeth in weeks, and from the looks of it, he hadn't. Darius finally picked up his pace and released all of his seeds inside of me, and I prayed that I wouldn't get pregnant by him. He collapsed on top of me breathing hard as hell like he had actually done something. My vagina felt like it was on fire, because it didn't get wet at all while he was inside of me.

"Shit girl, you still got that bomb ass pussy." he said. He slowly got off of me then kissed me in my mouth again.

"I'm getting some of that good shit every day, so be ready." he told me while leaving out of the basement. I wiped my tears and decided that I wasn't going to shed any more tears, ever. Crying won't do shit about this situation. Crying won't get me out of this small ass basement either. I just needed my body to heal all the way, and then it was going to be on from there. I was finding a way up out of here. And when I did, all of the people who hurt me was going to feel me. They didn't even know who they were fucking with, but that was okay. They'd know soon enough.

Chapter Four

Los

    This could not be life right now. I was just sitting on the couch not believing the phone call I had just received. Tammy was murdered. Not only was she murdered, but she was murdered while my son was in the house too. Tammy was a sweet girl. Yeah, it was messed up what she did to Londyn, but other than that, she was sweet. She didn't have any enemies because she wasn't one of those girls who ran off at the mouth.

    Tammy's mom had called me crying saying that she found her body on the kitchen floor with two bullets in her head. Someone had come through the back door because the glass was shattered when she got there. She also said that C.J was screaming at the top of his lungs when she got there too. She had C.J right now until I could get myself together to go get him from her. I guess he was going to be living with me now.

    It hadn't even a whole month since Alani died and now my baby's mother was dead too. This was just too much. I didn't want to plan another funeral, but being that she was my son's mother, it was only right. I told her mom not to worry about anything because I had it. I didn't even realize how long

I had been sitting on the couch until my phone rang and brought me out of my thoughts.

"Hello." I angrily spat into the phone.

"Carlos? What's the matter? Why do you sound like that?" Londyn asked. I sighed and decided to tell her what happened. I mean, Tammy was her friend too.

"Tammy was murdered."

"Oh my goodness, are you serious? When? Who would do such a thing? Are you okay? Do you need me to come over?" she asked question after question. I just really wanted to be alone right now.

"Nah, I'm good. I'm good." I let her know.

"Are you sure? I know you just lost Alani. I can't even imagine how you're feeling right now." I didn't say anything back for a while.

"I'm good." I repeated trying not to start crying like a little bitch.

"Carlos... I hear you, but I know you're over there hurting. Send me your address, and I'll come keep you company. You don't need to be alone at a time like this because that's only going to make you feel worse than you already do." she let me know. She was right. I ended the call and sent her the address to my condo.

I popped the two pills that were on the table then started rolling a blunt. That was all I did lately. Smoke, drink, and pop pills. I didn't even care about shit right now. I knew business was good thanks to Ali and Langston. They knew I was going through some shit right now. I just needed to get myself together.

There was a knock at the door, and I already knew that it was Londyn. I lit the blunt then got up to answer the door. It seemed like Londyn looked better and better every time I saw her. She had on a white romper that was showing off her thick ass thighs, her breasts were sitting up nicely, and today, she had on a burgundy wig that stopped right above her ass, which looked like it was getting bigger. She threw her arms around my neck, and she smelled like *Pure Seduction* by Victoria's Secret. That was Alani's favorite perfume to wear. I quickly stepped away from her because the smell was bringing back thoughts of Alani, and I was already having a hard time holding myself together.

"How are you holding up?" she asked. I felt the effects of the pills, and I just walked away leaving her at the door. I wasn't the same person whenever I popped pills, but I didn't care. I needed something stronger than weed and liquor, and I knew damn well I wasn't about to be sniffing cocaine up my damn nose.

"Carlos?" she asked.

"What?" I snapped.

"I asked you a question and you just walked away from me." she said like I had hurt her feelings or some shit.

"That means I don't feel like answering the damn question. You're a smart girl, Londyn acting like it." She

27

didn't say anything else. She just sat down on the couch beside me and watched me as I smoked.

"I'm so sorry you're going through this." she said rubbing my back.

"Go get me the Hennessy out of the kitchen." She did what she was told and came back with a half drunken bottle of Hennessy. She handed it to me then sat down on the couch again.

"Do you need anything?" she asked.

"I need for you to shut the fuck up for a minute, damn. Your ass is talking too damn much. Let a nigga get fucked up in peace!"

"Why the fuck are you being so rude?" she finally asked standing up.

"Bitch this is my crib, I can do whatever the fuck I want!"

"Why would you even call me over here of you're gonna be a complete asshole?"

"Shut the fuck up and come suck this dick. That's what you want right? That's why you've been calling and checking up on me? Cause you want some dick again? You think that since Alani is out of the picture that I'll come running back to you?" I asked then took two shots of Henny.

"What? No, Carlos! I wanted to know how you were holding up! I still love you, why can't you see that?" I didn't give a fuck about none of this shit that she was talking about.

28

My dick was hard, and she wasn't doing shit but running her mouth. I pulled my dick out and looked at her.

"It's not going to suck itself." I told her. She stood there for a minute before she finally decided to drop to her knees. She swirled her tongue around the tip first before actually taking my whole dick into her mouth. I had forgotten how good of a head game Londyn had. She wasn't on Alani's level, but she was up there.

"Shit." I grunted, forcing her head further down. I could hear her gagging, but I didn't give a fuck. I started fucking her mouth like it was a pussy.

"You better not throw up on my shit, bitch." I said. She had tears in her eyes, but she knew better than to try to stop. I felt my nut rising so I started going even faster.

"Fuckkkkk!" I yelled. I pulled out of her mouth and nutted all over her face. I could tell by the look on her face that she wasn't feeling what I had just done. Too bad I didn't give a fuck though. After my nut, I was tired as hell. I heard Londyn talking to me, but I didn't pay it no attention as I drifted off to sleep right there on the couch.

I woke up the next morning still on the couch. I guess the pills made me tired as hell. I didn't even remember falling asleep. Londyn was sleeping on the couch beside me, and I didn't like that shit at all. She should've taken her ass home last night once she saw that I was sleep. My dick was still out and everything.

I got up off of the couch to go relieve my bladder. I was hungry as fuck, and Londyn needed to either cook me some breakfast or get the hell out. After I had finished up in the bathroom, I went back into the living room and picked up the liquor that I didn't finish last night. I hit Londyn hard as hell on her ass, and her eyes shot right open.

"Carlos what the fuck?" she yelled.

"Make me some breakfast. I'm hungry as fuck." I said, sitting back down on the couch and turning on the T.V.

"Don't you think it's a little too early for you to be drinking?" I ignored her ass and turned to ESPN. Alani would've already had my breakfast ready way before I even woke up. Londyn needed to shut the hell up and stop worrying about what the fuck I was doing.

"Get your ass in the kitchen." I demanded. I got up and went to my room to get some more pills. This is how I started my day now… with a few pills and a blunt. I popped the pills and used the liquor to swallow them. When I got back into the living room, Londyn was in the kitchen finally and I sat back down on the couch.

My thoughts drifted off to Alani and Tammy. They didn't deserve to die at such a young age. I didn't even get to have babies with Alani like I wanted to. I wanted at least four kids. I knew she would've been a good ass mother, too. It still didn't feel like she was really gone. I wished this was just a bad dream that I would wake up from, and then Alani would be right there lying next to me in bed. I still remember the look of hurt on her face when she saw me, Tammy, and C.J at the mall. This all could've been prevented if I would've just told her. Shit, I didn't cheat on her with Tammy. We just had a child together. Alani would've been upset, but she would've come around.

"Carlos? Are you okay?" Londyn asked bringing me out of my thoughts.

"I'm good. Why do you keep asking me that shit?" I said getting irritated.

"Because you're crying. You can't be okay with tears falling down your cheeks." I didn't even know that I was crying until she said something about it. I wiped the tears away and finished all of my liquor. I instantly started rolling me a blunt. The way I was feeling right now, one wouldn't even be enough right now.

She sat there and stared at me the whole time I rolled the blunt. She was starting to get aggravating as fuck.

"Is the food ready?" I asked.

"Let me go check." I thought about popping another pill because the thoughts of Alani wouldn't stop, but Londyn came back into the living room with my plate. She made eggs, bacon, and pancakes. I ate the food like I hadn't eaten in days.

"Do you feel better?" she asked once I was finished.

"Yep." I got up to go handle my hygiene. I needed to get out of the house so I decided that I was going to go see what Ali was up to. I had enough of being around Londyn. She was starting to get annoying as hell. I knew she wanted

31

some dick, but I just wasn't even trying to go there with her. She's gonna start thinking that me and her are in a relationship again, and I didn't have time for that. I wasn't even looking for a relationship.

After my shower, Londyn was still in the living room. She looked up at me and I could tell that she wanted me to get all up in them guts. She even licked her lips. I chuckled and sat down on the couch.

"I'm about to go, so I'll get up with you later." I said.

"Where are you going? Why can't I go with you?" She had the nerve to ask.

"Because you're not my bitch, and I don't want you to. Like I said, I'll get up with you later." She knew damn well I didn't like being questioned. She really needed to go. She rolled her eyes then stood up.

"Whatever, Los. Don't hit me up when you want some pussy." she said. I just laughed at her.

"You'd be so happy if I did hit you up, but I got other bitches. Just like I had Tammy." She looked at me like she wanted to say something, but she decided not to. She grabbed her purse then stormed out of the condo. I didn't give a fuck about her little attitude. She could be mad all she wanted.

Once she was gone, I smoked another blunt then I was on my way to Ali's house.

Chapter Five

Ali

I laid on the bed and watched Draya's small boobs bounce up and down as she rode my dick. She had gotten a lot better at fucking, but she had no choice because that's all me and her did.

"You feel soooooo good, Ali!" she moaned grabbing both of her titties. She bit her bottom lip and threw her head back. Her sex faces were sexy as hell, and I was trying my hardest not to bust yet. I grabbed her hips to slow her down. She knew exactly what she was doing because she looked at me and started smirking.

"Shit girl, slow down." I said. My phone started ringing so I reached over to answer it. Of course, it was Trina.

"What's up?" I asked.

"Damn Ali, have you forgotten about me and your child? I haven't talked to you in weeks!" she yelled. I smacked my lips. Draya grilled me because she knew I was on the phone with another female.

"I'm a grown ass man. I can do whatever I want." I told her. Draya propped herself up on both of her feet and placed her hands on my chest. She started riding me like her life depended on it.

"Ohhhhhhh Ali!" she yelled. I knew exactly what she was doing. She wanted Trina to hear us fucking. I didn't want to entertain her being messy, but she was feeling too damn good.

"Ali, are you fucking another bitch while we're on the phone?!" Trina yelled.

"Fuck, you about to make me bust." I said, ignoring everything that Trina was saying. I sat the phone down so that I could fuck Draya back. She wasn't about to out fuck me. I flipped her around so that she was on all fours, and I showed no mercy as I pounded her.

"Wait, Ali! Shitttttt, it's so big!" I bit my lip so that I wouldn't yell out like a bitch. She didn't help when she starting squeezing her pussy muscles.   "I'm cumming, baby!" she yelled, and I was right behind her. I released all of my seeds inside of her then collapsed on the bed. My phone started ringing again, and I already knew it was Trina.

"What?" I asked annoyed with her already.

"Why the fuck would you answer the phone while you're having sex with someone else?" she asked. I could hear it in her voice that she was crying, and I didn't understand why.

"Be happy that I answered the phone at all for your ass. Now what do you want?"

"I want you. I haven't seen or heard from you in weeks, then you answer the phone while fucking another bitch. What the fuck, Ali?"

"Man chill with all that crying shit. I'll be over there later." I said then ended the call. Draya sat up and looked at me.

"That was so disrespectful." she said folding her arms across her chest.

"Fuck you talking about?"

"You answered the phone to talk to another female while we're having sex, then you're talking about going to see her later? What, are you gonna fuck her too?" Why the fuck were these bitches trippin' today?

"Shit, I might. I don't know yet." I said.

"Are you serious?! So you're just going to cheat on me like that?" she yelled.

"Cheat? I'm not in a relationship with no one so I can fuck whoever I want."

"So we're not in a relationship?" she asked with tears in her eyes.

"Hell naw. When the hell did I tell you that we were making things official?" She just sat there and stared at me. This is something that I didn't understand about females. They try to force us into relationships.

"You moved me into your house, you're always giving me money, you're always buying me nice things, you bought me a new car, and you've been dicking me down nonstop for almost a month now. Now you want to tell me that we're not in a relationship?" She was still yelling, and the shit was starting to piss me off.

"You need to calm the fuck down. If I knew doing all of this would've been a problem, then I wouldn't have done it. This is what I get for being nice to y'all bitches." I said getting up to go to the bathroom.

"OH, SO NOW I'M A BITCH?!" she yelled, but I closed and locked the bathroom door so that she couldn't get in. I wasn't in the mood for this shit. Females make shit so complicated. Why can't we just fuck and leave it at that? Why do they always want to put a title on shit and complicate things? Draya banged on the door until I got out of the shower. She was really about to piss me off.

As soon as I walked out of the bathroom, I was met with a right hook to my jaw. Draya was still standing there naked and looking like a mad woman. I held my jaw where she had just punched me and just looked at her.

"I will not be treated like I'm just some hoe!" she yelled. I pushed her on the bed and quickly got dressed. If I stayed in this room with her, I was going to end up putting my hands on her ass and I didn't want that. As soon as I was dressed, I walked downstairs. I needed a blunt and something to drink. I was shocked to see Los sitting on the couch smoking and watching T.V.

"What's up, nigga? When the hell did you get here?" I asked walking over to him. His eyes were bloodshot and low as hell. I knew he was high off of something else other than weed.

"Bout an hour ago. I had to get out of the house. I was going crazy in there." I could see it in his eyes that he was hurting, but shit, I was too. Alani was like a sister to me, and on top of all that, I was still missing Lena. I was hoping she would just come back and we could move on but I was starting to doubt that.

"Don't you fucking walk away from me when I'm talking to you!" Draya yelled coming down the stairs. She was still naked as the day she was born, and I wasn't feeling this shit at all. I didn't know why the hell she was still trippin'.

"Bruh, get the fuck on!" I yelled. She was swinging at me but she was missing. I pushed her into the wall and she fell. She looked shocked that I had done that, but I really didn't even care. I grabbed her by her weave and drug her out of the house. I didn't even care that she was naked. She should've thought about that shit before she came down here trying to start shit.

"Ali!" she yelled banging on the door. I walked to the table and grabbed my pistol. I opened the door and aimed it right at her head.

"Bitch, you got ten seconds to get the fuck on before I put one on ya head!" I yelled. Her eyes got big as hell and she took off running. That bitch was out of her damn mind today. Walking back into the house, Los sat on the couch laughing at me.

"Shut the fuck up. This shit ain't funny." I said sitting on the couch beside of him.

"You always get stuck with the crazy bitches. Why was she trippin anyway?"

"Because I told Trina I would be over there later. She started trippin and shit and saying how I'm so disrespectful. I told her ass we ain't in no damn relationship so I could do whatever the fuck I wanted. This bitch punched me in my damn jaw. That's when I came down here because I was liable to kill her ass if I would've stayed in that room." He passed me the blunt and I gladly took it.

"You didn't have to put her ass out naked." he laughed.

"Yes I did. Now she knows not to fuck with me. I don't know who the last nigga was that she was fucking with, but he had to be a pussy or something. She had me fucked up though."

"Tammy's dead." he said out of nowhere.

"Tammy who?"

"My baby mama." He put his hands over his face and I already knew he was trying his hardest not to start crying.

"How did she die?"

"Man, somebody murdered her. Shot her twice in the head while my son was upstairs. They could've easily killed him too, but they didn't. I can't even imagine who would do something like that to her. She didn't mess with nobody." I didn't know what to say. I was in a state of shock. I couldn't help but feel for him though because he had just lost his girl, and now his baby moms is gone too.

"Damn, that's fucked up. How did you find out?" I asked not really knowing what to say to him.

"Her mom called me and told me. Everything is just all fucked up. Now my son has to grow up without a mother. I don't even know if I can be a good father to him right now. I'm not right in the head." He shook his head then reached into his pocket and pulled out two pills.

"You got some Vodka or something?" he asked. I pointed to the bar and he made his way over there. I watched him as he took both pills and then he drank half the bottle. My cousin was really going through it right now and there wasn't shit I could do to make him feel better.

"Man, I'm gon' holla at you later. I need to find some shit to get into." Hehe said stumbling back over to the couch,

"Man, hell nah. You just drunk half the damn bottle, and I watched you pop some pills that I'm pretty sure weren't headache pills. Sit your ass down for a minute." I told him.

"Nigga, fuck you. I'm good. I know how to control my damn liquor. I'll hit you up later." he said, then walked out of the house. I felt bad that I just let him leave the house in his condition, but he's a grown ass man. I can't make him do something that he doesn't want to do.

I decided that I didn't want to be sitting in the house all day either, so I was gonna show up to Trina's house early. Shit, she probably wasn't doing anything anyway but flapping her gums to them bitches she calls friends and shit. I guess I would call Draya later, but she needed to learn how to act.

39

Pulling up to Trina's house, I saw that there was an all-black Benz in the driveway. I didn't pay it no mind though. I just figured it was one of her female friends or some shit. I walked up to the door and unlocked it since I had a key. I was still paying all the bills and shit since Trina acted like she couldn't get a job.

It was quiet when I walked into the house. The T.V was off but there were two plates at the table with half eaten breakfast food on them. I didn't think too much of that because Trina always acts like she doesn't know how to clean up. Shaking my head, I made my way into her bedroom and imagine my surprise when I saw her and some nigga fucking. He was hitting it from the back so I just stood there and watched with a smirk on my face.

"Ohhh Quincy, I'm about to cummmmm!" she yelled. This was so interesting to me. She was always on my dick, but she had a whole nigga that she was fucking in the house that I pay the bills in. I chuckled which caused both of them to stop and look at me.

"Ali! W-What are you doing here?" she stuttered trying to cover herself up with the blankets.

"I told you I was coming by, but I see you're busy." I laughed.

"It's not what you think. I swear it isn't."

"So did you try to pin the baby on him, too?" After I said that, he looked at her like wanted to kill her.

"You told this nigga that he was the father of my seed? The fuck is wrong with you?" he asked.

"Quincy…" she said but he cut her off.

"Why the fuck am I still paying all your bills then? Get this nigga to pay them!" he yelled getting out of bed and putting his clothes on. He was mad as hell.

"Nigga, I pay all the bills up in this bitch. This house is in my name." I let him know. He looked at me then back at her and laughed.

"So you just been using me to get my money, huh? Let me know when that baby gets here. I want a DNA test." he said, then left out of the house. He even slammed the door on his way out like a bitch. I just stood there laughing at Trina's ass. She really tried to play me and that nigga.

"Why are you even here?" she asked with tears running down her cheeks.

"I can't come and see my baby mama?" I asked then laughed. This whole thing was funny to me.

"Just leave." she told me. I looked at this bitch like she was crazy.

"You want me to leave? Leave the house that I pay all the bills in? Leave the house that's in my name? Nah bitch, you got me fucked up. You know what? How about you leave. Get all the shit that I didn't pay for and get the hell out my shit."

"What? Are you serious right now? Where the hell am I going to go?" she cried.

"Back to the hood to live with your mom and sister. Hurry the fuck up, too. I might give this house to my new bitch I'm fucking." I walked out of the room and went to sit down on the couch. I felt like I was being an asshole today, but at the same time, I didn't really care. I guess it was time to go back to the old me. Fuck bitches and get money.

Chapter Six

Alani

It had been two months since I'd been down in this basement. Well, that's how long I think it's been. Every day, it was the same shit. Darius was raping me, Londyn was beating me for no reason at all, and Jasmine was still trying to be my friend. I still wasn't feeling her trying to talk to me, but after she told me what Londyn and Darius had did to her, I started to feel bad. She even told me that she would help me get out of this damn prison I was in.

She would come down here every day once they left the house to give me something to eat. If it wasn't for her, I probably would've died from starvation. I was actually glad that she found it in her heart to help me out. She even apologized for making me lose my baby all those years ago when we were fighting over Darius. She was about eight months pregnant when she lost her baby, and I couldn't even imagine going through something like that. Feeling your baby move every day, to not feeling a baby there at all. It was so sad.

The door opened, and Jasmine walked in with a plate of breakfast like always. She handed it to me then sat at the end of the bed.

"They're both gone for the day. You have a good amount of time to change clothes and leave. Do you know where you're going to go?" she asked. I didn't know where I was going to go actually. I just wanted to get out of Miami. My mind instantly drifted off to Lena and how much I missed her crazy ass. The last I heard, she was supposed to be going to her mom's house. That was all the way in Jacksonville, though.

"I'm thinking about going to Jacksonville. There isn't anything left for me here. Once I get myself together, I'm coming back, and Londyn and Darius are going to be in for a rude awakening." I said, meaning every word. I was going to save Carlos for last though. I wanted to be in his house and meet up with him face to face so I could figure out why he did me so dirty.

"I'm getting out of here too. They'll probably try to kill me once they find out that I let you go free, so I'm taking my mom and my kids, and we're leaving Miami too. I'm starting to wish I would've never married Darius." she said shaking her head.

"Girl, I feel you on that one." She got up to leave and I finished my food. I didn't know when the next time I was going to eat was going to be so I had to make this last. Jasmine came back downstairs and handed me some clothes.

"These are mine, and I don't know if you can fit them or not, but I know you're tired of being naked." she said, handing the clothes to me. She was so right. I was so tired of being naked. Darius had stripped me from my hospital gown and left me like this. He said that it was much easier to get to me if I'm already naked.

I slowly stood up and carefully put the shirt over my head. It was a little tighter than I would've preferred but it was better than nothing. I slid the sweatpants on right after and sat back down on the bed. My body was still sore from all the beatings and being raped every day, but I was determined to get out of here.

"Follow me." she said. I slowly followed behind her as we went upstairs. This was actually a nice house. We walked into the master bedroom, and she went into the closet. Moments later, she came out with guns and money.

"You'll need this." she said, handing me stacks of money and two guns. She got a plastic bag to put everything in.

"Take my car. Once you get to where you're going, get rid of it." She handed me some keys and went back downstairs. I didn't know where the hell they got all this money from, but I wasn't complaining because I didn't have shit.

"Be safe. I hope you make it to where you're going." she said, once I got inside of the car. It wasn't one of the fancy cars I was used to; it was a 2014 Nissan Altima.

"Thank you for everything. I really don't know if I would've made it out without you." I told her. She smiled at me and turned around to walk back into the house. I rolled down the passenger window and shot her twice in her back. Once she fell to the ground, I quickly got out of the car and ran over to her. I put another bullet in the back of her head, then ran in the house. She left her half of the money and guns on the bed. I took it, then I was out of the house and back inside of the car.

I know what I did was fucked up, but I didn't trust that bitch. Yeah, she helped me to get out of that basement, but she could've easily told them where I was going. She had to go. I felt bad because she had kids, and they wouldn't grow up with a mother, but oh well. This is how it had to be. She couldn't say shit to Darius and Londyn if she was dead right? I backed out of the driveway and was on my way to Jacksonville.

I felt like it took forever for me to finally get to Lena's mom's house. I was glad when I finally made it though. I was a little nervous because I didn't know what to expect. I slowly turned the car off and got out of the car. It was night time outside, so I hurried to the front door to ring the doorbell. It took a while, but the door finally swung open, and sure enough, it was Lena standing there with an annoyed look on her face.

"Hey." I said, shyly. She was looking at me like I had grown two heads. She didn't say anything either. She just looked at me.

"Lena, who's at the door?" her mom said, walking up behind her. When she saw me, she froze too. What in the world?

"Mommy, you see her too right?" Lena asked her mom.

"Oh my goodness." Lena's mom Patricia pulled me in for a hug. She hugged me like I was dying or something.

"How are you here right now?" Lena asked me.

"I drove."

"No, how are you alive? You died. I was at your funeral. We both were. We sat in the back so that no one would recognize us, then we came straight back here." Now I was confused. What the hell did they mean they were at my funeral? I've been in a damn basement for almost three months.

"Died? No, I got kidnapped. I escaped today." They let me in the house and I went to go sit down on the couch.

"Well, it was all over the news. You got into a really bad car accident and died at the hospital. You didn't have an open casket though." Lena said. I told her everything that had happened to me after the car crash. Once I was finished, she was ready to go back to Miami and finish the job for me.

"I can't believe Carlos would do something like that. He couldn't have just broken up with you? Niggas ain't shit man, I swear. I can't wait for you to go back down there and get your revenge. I'm definitely coming back for that shit." she ranted. I was so happy to be out of that basement though.

I was glad to be around Lena. It had been way too long since I had last seen her.

"Why did you come back to Jacksonville, anyway?" I asked.

"I just had to get away. I had lost myself in a man, and I needed to get back to normal. I didn't plan on staying down here for so long, but I did. I just don't want to go back and see his stupid face again. All my feelings are probably going to come rushing back." she said.

"You're going to have to face him one day eventually. Even if y'all don't ever get back together. He was a wreck when you left him."

"Enough about me, did you hear that Tammy got killed?" she asked, getting up to go into the kitchen.

"Who the hell is Tammy?" She came back with a bottle of water and handed it to me.

"Carlos' baby mama." I rolled my eyes.

"Shit, he's probably the one that killed her. Him and Londyn." I shook my head at how grimy that nigga was. I couldn't believe that I had fallen in love with him either.

"That's so fucked up though. I saw it on Facebook. Everyone was tagging her in statuses like she was going to be able to see them and shit." she chuckled.

"The only person I feel bad for is that baby, because his daddy is a grimy ass nigga." I didn't want to talk about Carlos unless it had something to do with me killing his bitch ass. He fucked with the wrong bitch when he tried to get me killed. Darius fucked with the wrong bitch by raping me every day, and Londyn.. well, I planned on doing some gruesome shit to her ass. By the time I was finished with her, she was going to be begging me to kill her stupid ass.

I stayed up late as hell talking to Lena. I missed her so much, and I was glad I was able to be around her again. I wasn't letting her leave me like this ever again. I couldn't help but wonder if Carlos even felt bad about what he did to me or if he even missed me a little bit.

"Have you talked to Jaxon?" she asked. I shook my head no.

"I haven't talked to anyone except you and your mom. I want to call him and tell him that I'm alive, but I think I'm going to just wait and show my face when I go back to Miami. When he finds out what Carlos did, he might end up back in jail again, and I really don't want that." I let her know.

"I feel you. Well, tomorrow, we're getting that hair done and those nails. Lord only knows what those feet are looking like. Then, we're going out to celebrate. My bitch is back and ready for whatever." I rolled my eyes.

"Girl bye, my hair is fine. It just needs to be washed." She looked at me like I was crazy.

"Bitch please; that shit is so matted. You're going to need more than Dr. Miracle." She was probably right, though. In the small ass bathroom in the basement, there was no type of soap or shampoo, so I just did the best I could with just water.

"Whatever, bitch. It's time for a change anyway. I'm tired of my hair. I might cut it all off."

"Oh no, I can't have my bestie walking around looking bald. We'll find something that you want to do to your hair, and it's going to be flawless." She stood up and kissed me on my cheek.

"I'm going to bed. Be ready to wake up bright and early because we got shit to do. You can sleep in the guest room." she told me making her way up the stairs.

No matter how hard I tried, I just couldn't fall asleep. I was too busy thinking about the shit I wanted to do to Londyn, Carlos, and Darius. They're not even going to be expecting it when I come back either. I couldn't wait. I was getting anxious just thinking about it.

The next morning, Lena was in my room bright and early. She was looking good as hell like always. Her weave was down her back and curly, and she had on black leggings with a black cut off shirt. Her outfit was so simple, but she looked good. I looked at myself in the mirror and instantly felt bad.

My hair was curly, but it wasn't the cute curly. It was matted in so many places all over my head. My eyes weren't swollen, but under one of them, it was bruised real badly. My lip was busted, and I had cuts all down my face. I looked like shit compared to Lena.

"Don't look so down. You're still beautiful in my eyes." she told me. She sat me down on the toilet in the bathroom and put some concealer underneath my eye.

"See, now no one can even tell that it was ever there." she said. She was right, though. You couldn't even see the bruise. I felt a little better about going out, but not much. I took a quick shower and put on some of Lena's clothes. That's something else that I needed to do today. I needed to buy me a whole new wardrobe. I wasn't about to be walking around wearing other people's clothes.

When we got to the hair salon, there weren't that many people in there, and I was thankful for that. I didn't want too many people seeing me with my head looking like this. This was just straight up embarrassing.

"Hey Lena, who's your friend?" the girl at the front desk said eyeing me. I didn't like how she was looking at me like she had a problem with me.

"This is my best friend, Alani. She has an appointment with Kim." Lena said. The girl chuckled and mumbled something under her breath that sounded like "She needs more than that."

"Excuse me? What was that? Do you have something that you need to say?" I asked.

"If I had something to say, I would damn sure say it." she said with an eye roll.

"Dumb bitch." I said, walking away with Lena. I didn't know why the hell she had a problem with me, but I wasn't feeling that shit at all.

"Damn Lani. Calm down." Lena said once we were away from that bitch.

"Fuck that hoe. I didn't do shit to her, and she's looking at me and rolling her eyes like I'm fucking her man or something."

"No, that's just how Leslie is. She comes off as rude to everyone." Lena defended her. I waved her off and sat down in the chair.

"So what can I do for you today?" Kim asked me.

"I need something new. I'm tired of having long hair, and I'm tired of it being this color. I want something makes me look like a bad bitch." I told her.

"I know exactly what to do." she said. I was at that damn hair salon for about two hours. There was a lot of my hair on the floor, and I didn't even know how I felt about that. It kind of felt good not having all of that hair anymore.

"And we're finished." Kim said, turning me around in the mirror so that I could see myself. I had to say that I was shocked at how good my hair looked. She had cut it shoulder-length and dyed it burgundy. I looked good as hell.

"Damn bitch, you look like you just stepped right out of a magazine. You should've been dyed your hair this color." Lena said. We paid Kim and were now on our way to get our nails done. On the way out, that Leslie bitch looked even more bothered with me. I blew her simple ass a kiss and kept it moving.

"You're probably going to find you a new boo tonight." Lena smiled.

"Oh no, I'm not looking for a new nigga. If anything, I'm trying to stay as far from niggas as possible. Niggas ain't good for shit but a little piece of dick." I told her.

"Just because one nigga fucked you over doesn't mean that all niggas are going to do the same thing." I rolled my eyes.

"It was two niggas that was out to get me, and I really don't care. Fuck all of them. I might fuck a nigga, but that's as far as it's going. Ain't no relationships happening for me anytime soon." Lena didn't say anything else about it. She knew my mind was set, and I didn't plan on changing it. Fuck these niggas.

After getting our nails done, we went to the mall. I swear, we hit up every damn store that was in the bitch. I had so many damn bags, it was ridiculous. Lena had some bags, but she didn't have as much as me. She looked tired as hell, but I still wanted to shop.

"I guess I could always come back later since you want to be a crybaby." I told her.

"Shut up, bitch. We've been in this damn mall for almost four hours now. My feet and back hurt. I'm hungry as hell too."

"Stop complaining. But, I could use some Chinese food right about now." We made our way to the food court and both got Chinese food.

"What's up, Lena?" I heard a voice say as we made our way to our table.

"Hey Legend." Lena said giving him a side hug.

"Who's your friend? I'm shocked she can deal with your mean ass."

"Boy shut up. This is my best friend, Alani. Alani, this is Legend." I looked up at the man Lena was talking to, and I was shocked. He was fine as hell. He was at least 6'2, and he had sexy ass dark skin. I could see all of the tattoos that were all over his arms, and his beard was a medium length. All the hair on his face connected perfectly. His eyes were dark brown, and I felt like he was looking through my soul. He had one of those haircuts that was tapered on the sides, and it was a small little fro on top. He was wearing a pair of gray sweat pants and I could see his massive print. I couldn't even stop myself from staring at his gorgeous ass.

"It's nice to meet you, Alani." Legend said, taking my hand and kissing it. I couldn't help but blush and smile at him.

"I'll see you two around. Hopefully, really soon." He winked at me then walked away.

"Bitch what the fuck was that?" Lena asked once we sat down.

"Huh? What you talking about?"

"Don't play stupid. You was staring at his ass like you wanted to suck his dick right here."

"I did. Who is he?"

"That's Leslie's boyfriend. They've been together for like five years now." I rolled my eyes at Leslie's name.

"He was looking at me mighty hard."

54

"And so were you. He's taken so don't bother." she said.

"You and that Leslie bitch friends or some shit?" I asked, feeling a little jealous for some reason.

"I mean yeah, we hang out from time to time. She's actually a really cool person to hang out with." I rolled my eyes again.

"Oh." was all I said.

"I know what you're thinking, but don't worry. No one could ever replace my bestie." I smiled at her, even though I wasn't thinking that at all. I was thinking about riding Legend's dick from the back. Shit, Leslie may have been Lena's friend, but I didn't owe that bitch any kind of loyalty. I had to see what his dick game was like, and I couldn't wait to find out either.

Chapter Seven

Londyn

I spent my whole day with Los, and I couldn't have been happier. He even took me to the mall and was buying me shit like I was his girlfriend. I was getting all types of looks from bitches, but I knew they were just hating. They wanted what I had and they couldn't get it. It felt good as hell walking with him by my side, and I tried to hold his hand, but he wasn't really feeling that.

"I'm going to go to the bathroom before we leave." I told Los. He just nodded his head and felt around in his pocket. I didn't know what it was that he was looking for, but it didn't concern me. I just needed to get to a bathroom and fast.

After I released my bladder, I washed and dried my hands and made my way back to Los. I wasn't too happy when I saw a bitch smiling all up in his face. I didn't know who this hoe was, but he was smiling back. I watched them as he put her number in his phone and instantly got pissed. Who the fuck did this bitch think she was? I stormed over to the both of them and stood beside of Carlos.

"Hey, who is this?" I asked. The two dollar hoe looked at me and had the nerve to roll her eyes. Her weave was stiff as hell, and she looked like she still shopped at Rainbow. This bitch ain't have shit on me even on my worse day.

"None of your damn business." Los snapped. I looked at him, and he had an annoyed look on his face like I had done something wrong.

"I'll be waiting for your call, Los." the girl said seductively then walked away. He stared at her ass until she was no longer in eyes reach. How disrespectful!

"Let's go." he said walking off.

"Nigga, what the fuck was that? How are you just gonna disrespect me like that?" I asked. I was ready to fight him and this bitch. They both had me fucked up.

"Fuck is you talking about?" he asked. We got into his car, and I made sure to slam the door.

"You're just going to have that hoe in your face like you're not at the mall with me? Then when I ask you who this bitch is, you tell me it's none of my business? What the fuck?" I yelled.

"You need to calm that shit down! You're not my bitch. You're just a bitch I'm fucking. Therefore, you shouldn't be questioning shit I do." he said through gritted teeth. He pinched the bridge of his nose then reached into his glove compartment to get out a bag full of weed and pills. He pulled two pills out and popped them.

"You just took two of those right before we came to the mall. Don't you think you need to slow down?" I asked.

"I need the whole bag fucking with your stupid ass." He turned the music all the way up and sped out of the parking lot. Ever since this whole Alani thing has happened, he's been treating me like dog shit. I didn't understand why he's so damn mad at me. I haven't done shit to his ass but try to be there for him. Yeah, I'm the reason he thinks she's dead in the first place, but he doesn't know that.

Carlos pulled up in front of my house. He didn't even put the car in park.

"You're not coming in?" I asked.

"Nah, I got some shit to do." he said.

"Like what? Go fuck that two dollar hoe that you just met?" I snapped.

"Yep." he said lighting a blunt. He said it like he didn't even give a fuck about my feelings. I knew he wasn't lying either. It made my heart sink to the pit of my stomach. For the past two months, he's been with me. Fucking my brains out and spending the night with me. Now all of a sudden he wants to go fuck someone else? What the hell? I didn't say anything else to him. I just got my ass out of the car and walked up the driveway to the door. This rude ass nigga didn't even wait to see if I made it in the safely. He pulled right the fuck off. I just shook my head and walked into the house. As soon as I sat down on the couch, my phone started ringing.

"Yes, Darius?" I asked already annoyed. Darius called me all the time wanting some pussy, but now that I'm fucking Los again, I didn't have time for Darius' whack ass sex.

"Yo, we got a problem. A huge problem. Get to my house now." he said, then ended the call. I wasn't in the mood for Darius right now. Knowing him, he didn't even want shit. He just needed a way to get me to his house. Shit, he had a wife. I didn't understand why he just wouldn't fuck that bitch.

I took my sweet little time going to Darius' house. I took a shower, cleaned up my house a little bit, and I even painted my toenails. After that, I was bored so I finally decided to go see what it was that he wanted. It couldn't have been that important because if it was, he would've called me back again in the two hours it took me to get there.

Getting out of my car, I made my way into the house. I haven't messed with Alani today, and I wanted to beat her ass because of the way Carlos was treating me. Whenever he treated me badly, I took my anger out on her which was almost every day.

Walking into the house, I tripped over something hard and fell to the ground.

"What the fuck?" I yelled at Darius, who was just sitting there on the couch staring off into space. I thought my eyes were playing tricks on me when I saw Jasmine's lifeless body lying on the floor.

"Darius, what did you do?" I asked feeling myself getting mad because he's always doing some shit.

"She was dead on the porch when I got here, man. Alani did it. She's not in the basement anymore. The safe was open too and everything is gone."

"What?" I yelled. I took off running towards the basement. This could not be happening right now. When I opened the door, the basement was empty. I couldn't explain how I was feeling right now. There was no telling where Alani was and if she was going to snitch or not.

"Fuck!" I yelled. I knew I should've tied her ass up. This had to be Jasmine's fault because it was impossible for her to get out of the basement unless one of us opened the door. Jasmine got exactly what she deserved. I'm glad she's dead because she got annoying as hell. She was too damn scary, and I couldn't fuck with it.

I walked back upstairs and Darius was standing over Jasmine with a weird look on his face.

"What the hell are you doing? Why haven't you buried her somewhere or some shit?" I asked.

"You did this."

"Nigga how the fuck did I do it if I wasn't even here either?"

"She was the mother of my kids. My wife. She was a good person until you came along. You made us do all of this shit, and now she's dead." He looked up at me like he wanted to kill my ass.

"I didn't make y'all do shit. It's not my fault that your wife was a little scary bitch. She knew what the fuck we were doing. You did, too. I didn't make you fuck me. You did that. Don't go trying to blame me for shit. What you need to be doing is worrying about Alani. She killed your wife. The love of your life killed your wife." I laughed because I had rhymed. He didn't find anything funny though. I didn't care. I didn't feel bad at all. I just needed to find out where Alani was. I knew I should've killed her ass.

"Get rid of this body. I got shit to do." I told him then left the house. I couldn't believe this shit. I didn't let it show, but I was actually terrified that Alani was loose. I didn't know what she had planned, but I know she wasn't going to let us get away with what we had done to her. She might even go to Los and tell him everything. Then I knew for sure he would kill me right then and there.

I got in my car and just sat there for a minute. No one knew about this except Darius, Jasmine, and I so I couldn't go to anyone and ask them for advice. They'd probably call the police on me or some shit. This was why I didn't really have friends. I couldn't trust too many people. After a while of sitting there, I finally started my car and backed out of the driveway.

Maybe I should leave town. I thought to myself. But then I would be away from Los and I didn't want to do that. He was the whole reason I came up with this plan in the first place. Me and him were meant for each other, and we were going to be together forever. Right now, he was just mourning the loss of Alani; that's why he's being so mean to me. In a couple of months, he'll probably be asking me to marry him. I just need to find a way to get rid of Alani and fast.

Chapter Eight

Alani

It was now going on two weeks that I had been freed out of that damn basement, and I couldn't have been happier. Lena and I had basically been out every night in a club celebrating. I really don't even remember these last couple of weeks because by the end of the night, I'm always pissy drunk. I've been drinking way more than I usually do because I really just want to forget everything that had happened over the last couple of months.

"What you over there thinking about?" Legend asked me. Yeah, I was fucking him. The same day we seen him in the mall, we ran into him at the club too. My drunk ass was all over him and we exchanged numbers. We had sex the next day, and Lena was mad as hell about the whole thing, but I didn't care. She was only mad because she was friends with Leslie. I could care less about her though. She obviously didn't know how to keep a man happy. Otherwise, Legend wouldn't have me all up and through his home. The home that he and Leslie shared.

"Thinking about how I need some alcohol and a blunt." I told him. I was also smoking way more than I used to. I couldn't even start my day without smoking now. He looked at me and shook his head.

"It's eleven in the morning, and you're already talking about drinking?" he asked.

"It's never too early to drink. Shit, I'd love to drink something with the breakfast Leslie made for us. That was so kind of her." I said getting out of bed. I didn't even make it out of the bedroom door before he was pulling back and pushing me on the bed.

"This is my breakfast right here." he said spreading my legs apart and feasting on my kitty. Legend's head game was something serious.

"Mmmmmmm." I moaned while playing in his little curly fro. He stuck two of his fingers inside of me and I came instantly. He just had that effect on me. He didn't even let me come down or anything. He flipped me over on all fours and rammed his thick hard dick inside of me.

"Legenddddddd!"

"Shut the fuck up and take this dick." he demanded, slapping me on my ass. He pushed my head down into the pillows, and I gripped the sheets. This nigga never showed any mercy on me. He pulled out and slapped my pussy with his dick before putting it back in. He usually did that when he wasn't trying to nut too soon.

"Damn girl, this shit wet as hell." he said. I turned around so that I could look at him. He was looking down watching himself slide inside of me while biting his bottom lip. His sex faces were sexy as hell. I guess he felt me staring at him because he looked up at me. His dark eyes looked even darker, and I could tell he was biting his lip to keep from moaning. I, on the other hand, was screaming at the top of my lungs.

"You feel sooooo goooood." I moaned while still looking at him in his eyes. When I said that, he closed his eyes tight as hell.

"Shit, shit, shit." he whispered. He quickly pulled out then nutted all over my booty, then I fell onto the bed breathing hard as hell.

"You're always making me cum when I don't want to." he said laying down beside of me.

"Don't blame that shit on me. It's not my fault you're a minute man." I joked. He slapped me hard on the ass. "Ouch nigga, that shit hurts! Go get me a rag or something." He kissed me on my cheek then got up off of the bed. He came back with a warm rag and wiped me off. I was tired as hell now.

"Let's go eat." he said pulling me off of the bed. I forgot that I was even hungry. We made our way downstairs, and it looked like Leslie had cooked up a meal for a big ass family. She could cook though. For the past two weeks, I had been eating her food that she thinks she's only cooking for Legend.

"Why does she always cook so much food and it's only you eating?" I asked.

"I don't know. I have no idea what goes on in her head." He came up behind me and kissed me on my neck getting me horny all over again. We were still naked so I went and bent over the counter so he could enter me from the back again. He quickly caught on to what I was doing and came and slid right up in me.

"Shit, daddy." I moaned, while gripping the sides of the counter. His dick was huge and I loved every inch.

"You like this dick? Huh?" he asked slapping me hard on my ass.

"Yes, Daddy, I loveeee it!" He put my leg up on the counter and then put one of his hands around my neck. I loved this rough shit he was doing to me. I felt myself about to cum and then the front door opened.

"Babe? I'm home early!" she called out. She stopped in her tracks when she saw what we were doing.

"What the fuck, Legend?! You're fucking this bitch in our house?" she yelled. He pulled out of me and walked over to her. Dick swinging and all. I just stood there to see how this was going to play out.

As soon as he got close to her, she started swinging on him. She hit him one good time in his face, and he slapped the shit out of her. I think it was just a reflex. She fell to the floor and started crying her eyes out.

"How could you? Out of all people, you chose this trashy ass bitch?" she sobbed.

"Look Leslie, I'm not about to be too many more bitches." I said walking over to her.

"Fuck you, bitch. You could've just found your own damn man!" She stood up but I two pieced her ass and made her fall right back down. I went upstairs to put on my clothes because I already knew if I stayed any longer, I would end up killing this hoe.

I went back downstairs and they were still arguing. I shook my head at them two.

"Legend, call me later when you handle your situation." I told him. When I said that, Leslie tried to charge at me, but he caught her. I guess she didn't like what I had said, but I didn't care. She wasn't relevant anyway.

"Chill the fuck out." he told her. She looked at him like she was shocked and hurt. I chuckled and walked out of the house. I still had the car that Jasmine let me use and I really needed to get rid of it. I had plenty of money left over, but I needed more. I needed quick money. I knew exactly what it was that I was going to do too. I jumped in my car and sped off towards Lena's house.

Walking in the house, I could tell that Lena wasn't in a good mood at all. She looked like she was about ready to beat my ass or something.

"What's wrong with you?" I asked sitting down beside of her on the couch.

"I know I told you to leave Legend alone. Why the hell were you fucking him in their house? Damn Lani, I told you that she was my friend." Lena said shaking her head. I rolled my eyes because I was grown as hell. I could do whatever I wanted to do.

"Why are you mad at me? He's the one that started all of this. I didn't care where the hell we fucked at. Just as long as I got some dick, I was good. It's not my fault that she walked in on us fucking. She should've been at work anyway. Oh, and like you said. She's your friend. Not mine. I don't owe that bitch any type of loyalty. Fuck her and her feelings." Lena looked shocked after I said that.

"You wouldn't want someone to do that to you though."

"Yeah, I didn't want anyone to do that to me, but they did anyway. The only two niggas I ever loved fucked me over because there were other bitches in the damn picture. I could never have a nigga to my damn self. I was nothing but good to these niggas, and this is how they repay me. I never even thought about cheating on them while we were together. Too bad it wasn't the same for them. All I wanted was to be loved back, but no. I got kidnapped, beat, and raped. All because of a nigga. I'm sorry that I don't give a fuck anymore. That's how you end up hurt anyway." I told her. I went into my purse and pulled out a blunt that I already had rolled and lit it.

I felt like absolute shit now. I felt worthless. Like I was never good enough. Like I would never be good enough. I thought Carlos actually loved me, but he was plotting on killing me so that he could get back with Londyn. Darius was even helping him out. From my understanding, they didn't like each other. But they came together to try to kill me? What the hell did I do that was so damn bad? I was a nice girl. Especially in my relationships because I took them seriously. I couldn't believe that this was what my life had turned out to be.

"Lani? Are you crying?" Lena asked pulling me from my thoughts. I didn't even know that I was crying until I touched my face and felt the wetness. I quickly wiped my tears and got off of the couch. I walked into the kitchen and got a bottle of Paul Mason that I had bought the other night. I sat down at the kitchen table and just took the bottle to the head. I wanted to be drunk. I needed to be drunk. I needed these thoughts of Darius raping me to go away.

"Alani, you've been drinking nonstop for the past two weeks. I think you need to slow down." Lena said sitting down at the table in front of me.

"I need money. Get me a job at the club you work at." I said ignoring what she had just said.

"I mean, I can try. What do you want to do? Bartend?"

"No bitch, I want to dance. I want to get on stage and shake my ass for cash. I'm not going to be there long. I still got shit to handle in Miami."

"Well, go get dressed. We can go down there right now while no one is there. Don't punk out either." I chuckled at her.

"Punk out? Girl bye." I took another shot of my drink and then made my way to the guest bedroom so that I could shower and change clothes. I knew I had to look good when we went to the club, so after my shower, I put on a nude, strapless dress that hugged my body. My breasts were sitting up just right, and I didn't even have to put on a bra. I brushed my newly short hair that was still looking good as hell. I loved this shoulder length cut and the color was even better. I was thinking about dying it again before I went back to Miami, but I'm not sure yet. I put on a little bit of makeup because I really didn't need it. Then I sprayed on my Chanel No. 5 perfume so that I could smell good as hell. I put on a pair of black red bottom heels and then I made my way back down the stairs.

"Damn, bitch. We're just going to the club so that you can audition. You look like you're about to go to a photoshoot." Lena told me. I was looking good. I knew I was. I just wished I felt as good as I looked.

"You know, I have to make a good first impression."

"The way you're looking, you might not even have to audition. That ass is looking right in that dress." she said, and I just smiled at her. She always knew how to make me feel good about myself. That's why she was my bitch. We left out of the house and was on our way to the club.

The club that she danced at was big as hell. I wasn't expecting it to look like this at all. I instantly got a little nervous, but I was going to hit the bar before I did anything else. I smoked a blunt the whole way over here so my eyes were low as hell. Lena shook her head at me, but shit. Smoking made me feel better about the whole situation.

"This shit is nice as hell." I told Lena when we walked in. It looked like you could have a wedding here, it was so nice. It had three floors too. I walked my ass right over to the bar where a cute light-skinned girl was working. I told her to give me three shots of Patron and I downed all of them. I was still feeling a little nervous, so I asked for three more.

"Lani, chill. He's not gonna hire you if you're sloppy drunk and shit. Just relax." Lena said.

"I can't. I'm nervous. Where is he at anyway?"

"He said he was wrapping up a meeting. He'll be down here soon." I drank my last three shots and I started to loosen up a little bit. I was actually drunk as hell, but I was trying not to act like it.

"Sorry to keep you two beautiful ladies waiting." I heard from behind us. I turned around expecting the club owner to be an old fat white man, but I was shocked at what I was seeing. He was gorgeous. He was tall as hell with dreads that came to the middle of his back. He had beautiful brown skin and green eyes. I'd never seen a black person with green eyes before. He looked so damn good in his suit which I'm sure cost a lot of money. I could smell his cologne and it was making my kitty wet.

"Hey Juice, we're not in a hurry. We're on your time." Lena said. He looked at me and smiled showing me the perfect set of white teeth.

"You must be Alani." he said. I couldn't do anything but nod my head. He took my hand and kissed the back of it, and I thought that I was going to lose my damn mind.

"Follow me." he said. I got down off of the stool at the bar and slowly walked behind him. He took me up the stairs and into a room that looked like an office and lounge room at the same time. It even had a small stage with a pole on it and everything. He sat down on the couch and unloosened his tie. Damn, this man was fine as hell. Whoever his girlfriend is was lucky as hell.

"You can start whenever you're ready." he told me. He turned on some music and *Freak Hoe* by Future started playing. I couldn't control myself when that song came on so I wasted no time climbing on the small stage and putting on a show for him. The liquor had definitely taken over, because when my dress came up as I was twerking, I didn't even care. I even gave him a little lap dance. He couldn't keep his hands off of me, but I didn't mind. I wanted to rub all over his body too. I could feel his hard member through his pants as I ground on him. That didn't do anything but boost my confidence.

He finally cut the music off and just stared at me. The way he was looking at me was making me feel like I didn't do a good job or something.

"Did I not do good?" I asked. He didn't say anything. Instead, he picked me up and carried me over to his desk knocking everything off so he could sit me on it. He spread my legs apart then grabbed my chin and forcefully kissing me, and I could taste the mint on his breath. I didn't expect any of this to happen, and I knew it shouldn't have been happening.

"Wait." I tried to say because I knew exactly where this was going. He acted like he didn't hear me though. He started kissing me on my neck making me weak. Being that I was already high and a little drunk, I was extra horny. He slid my G-string to the side then inserted one of his fingers. Once he saw that I was dripping wet, he dropped his pants and entered me. I threw my arms around his neck so that I would have something to hold on to.

"Shitttttt." I moaned throwing my head back. The feeling that he was giving me was one that I wasn't getting from Legend. It was probably because Juice was way bigger than Legend. Juice let a small moan leave his lips then he pulled out of me. He helped me down from his desk and forced me to bend over. He had a handful of my hair as he pounded me from the back.

"Ohhhhh shittttttt!" I wanted to tell him to slow down, but that was the only thing that would come out. He slapped me hard on the ass then sped up his pace. My moans were loud as hell, and I hoped that no one could hear me. He finally pulled out and nutted on my butt. I was glad that it was over, but at the same time, I wanted more. This nigga had my feelings all over the place right now.

"Stay right here." he said then walked away. He came back with a warm rag and cleaned me up. I felt a little dirty. I didn't even know this nigga and here I was already giving up the goods to him. And on top of that, I was fucking Legend earlier. I shook my head at myself.

"I gotta go." I said, pulling my dress back down and quickly left out of his office before he could say anything. I needed to get out of this club. Maybe I could find another club to dance at or something. I just knew that it couldn't be this one. I didn't know if I was going to be able to control myself when I was around him.

I spotted Lena sitting at the bar so I went over to her and grabbed her by her hand pulling her out of the club.

"What happened? How did it go?" she asked once we got in the car. I didn't say anything. I just looked down.

"Alani! Please tell me you didn't fuck him." My silence was her answer. "I can't believe this shit. You were supposed to dance for him and that's it. How the hell did you end up doing this? That man is practically married!" she yelled at me like she was my mother. I just ignored her and looked out the window. Right now, men should be the last thing on my mind. I needed to focus on how I was going to get my revenge on these people who thought it was okay to do what they did to me. It was coming sooner than they thought. They aren't even ready for the wrath of Alani.

Chapter Nine

Jaxon

Ever since Alani's death, I haven't done anything but lay around the house. I couldn't even believe that her own best friend didn't even come to the funeral. They've been best friends since grade school, but Lena couldn't think about other people for once and come to the funeral. I bet if it was the other way around, Lani would've been front and center for Lena's funeral.

I wanted to be mad at Los but I couldn't. He wasn't the one that was driving the car, and it wasn't his fault that it started raining either. I just felt so empty because I was away from Alani for a whole five years, then when I finally get out of jail, she's taken from me. In a way, I'm still blaming Carla for that. If it wasn't for her, I wouldn't have been in jail for the last five years. I could've still been in my little sister's life before she died. This whole thing was just fucked up.

I haven't seen or spoken to Carla since the night of Alani's birthday party. I wanted to kill her that night, but I couldn't do that. I had just got out of jail and I really wasn't trying to go back no time soon. She had gotten my number and had been calling and texting me, but they all went unanswered. I didn't have nothing to say to that bitch. She did me dirty as hell. She claimed that she wasn't the one who set me up, but I didn't believe that shit at all. My phone started ringing, and of course it was Carla. I smacked my teeth and decided to answer it.

"Hello?" I said obviously annoyed.

"Jaxon? Oh my goodness, it's about time you answered your phone. I was starting to think that I had the wrong number." she said happily into the phone.

"You've been calling me for two months straight. What do you want?"

"I just wanted to see how you were holding up. I didn't get to talk to you at the funeral because you walked away so fast."

"I'm good. Everything is good over here. Is that all you wanted?" I asked ready to end this whole conversation.

"No...I... I miss you. I just really want to talk to you." I chuckled. After five years, she missed me? Man, these bitches really be on some other shit.

"Well talk."

"No, Jaxon. Can I come over and we talk?" I chuckled at her again. I couldn't trust this bitch as far as I could throw her and she wanted to come to my house? Where I lay my head at? Nah, that wasn't going to happen.

"Nah, that's not even about to happen. I can't trust you in my house. Knowing you, you might find some more shit to use to get me locked up again." I heard her sigh on the other end of the phone but I really didn't care. She couldn't possibly think that I was just going to let her back in and we were gonna ride off into the sunset or some shit. She's acting like what she did wasn't fucked up.

"Okay, Jaxon. Meet me at Olive Garden or something. I just really want to talk to you." I was quiet for a moment because I was debating on if I should really go talk to her ass or just stay my ass in the house. I decided that I was going to go just so that I could get out of the house. because I hadn't been out in a minute.

"Aight. I'll be there." I let her know then ended the call. I was wondering what type of lies she was going to tell me once I got there. I feel like that's all that came out of Carla's mouth. Lies, lies, and more lies.

I got out of the bed and went to get in the shower. I hadn't showered in the past two days being that all I was doing was laying here and being sad over my sister. I took a thirty-minute shower, then found something to wear. I didn't really care about how I was looking because it was just Carla that I was going to meet with. I wasn't trying to get me a new bitch, even though I could easily.

Pulling up to Olive Garden, I was almost certain that Carla was already here. She was always extra early for shit. I turned my car off and stepped out of it. I spotted Carla sitting at a table by herself scrolling through her phone. She was looking good as hell in a simple yellow sundress that had her titties spilling out of the top. Her hair was pulled into a nice looking bun, and she had some shit on her lips that made them shiny as hell. She looked up at me and smiled big as hell when I sat down at the table.

"I'm so glad you came. I thought you were gonna stand me up or something." she said putting her phone down.

"I told you I was coming right? Don't I always keep my word?"

"I mean, yeah… but you're still feeling some type of way…"

"Can you blame me?" I asked cutting her off.

"Look Jax, I know what I did was fucked up, but you have to realize that I was young, dumb, and in love. You were just using me anyway."

"Using you? Using you for what? I was making my own money, living in my own house. What could I possibly use you for? You sure as hell ain't have no money."

"Pussy." She had the nerve to say. I looked at her like her ass was stupid.

"I was using you for pussy? I was getting pussy thrown at me almost every day. I don't have to use no bitch for pussy. Didn't have to do it then, and I damn sure don't have to do it now." I let her know.

"Yeah, I know you were getting pussy thrown at you every day. That's why your ass was cheating on me." She had a look on her face like she knew some shit I didn't. I never cheated on her ass. I had plans to make her my wife and the mother of my children. I was too happy when I got her ass pregnant. I was going in raw on purpose. I knew what the fuck I was doing. She lost the baby and blamed it on me because I was stressing her out because I wasn't home enough for her.

"Cheating on you with who?" I asked because this was all new to me.

"I don't know who the bitch was. I just knew she had long curly hair and I saw you and her walking into your apartment one night."

"Walking her into my apartment? The only people I had in my house was you and Alani. You must've been trippin' that night." I knew for a fact I didn't have no bitch in my apartment. The only females I really talked to were Carla and Alani.

"I wasn't trippin'! I know exactly what I saw that night and that was you and her. Mia was the one who let me know that you be having bitches all up and through your apartment. I had to come and see it for myself. I was so embarrassed and hurt that night. That's why I did what I did to you. But, you really can't blame me." She was trying to justify what she did by blaming it on me when I never cheated on her to begin with.

"So since you thought you saw me cheating on you, you set me up and get me locked up for five years? Then you're sitting here like what you did was okay. I never cheated on you, Carla. I was ready for you to have my baby but you see how that ended. The girl I was bringing into my house was Alani. She would spend all day with Lena and then come home at night. I was the one that was picking you up. You didn't even know that I had a sister." I chuckled and shook my head at her.

"You never told me about her."

"Because you didn't ask. Just like you didn't ask me about the girl you saw me walking into the apartment with. You don't want to come to me like a woman. You want to be childish and set me up so that I would be in jail. You couldn't possibly care about me. No bitch is going to do that. I don't give a fuck how mad they are. I should put my foot up your ass for what you did. That's some fucked up shit, Carla. But I'm glad you did it. You let me see the real you. I dodged a bullet." I smiled at her, and her face dropped. I could tell that I had hurt her feelings, but how the fuck was I supposed to feel. The woman I loved set me up over some shit that wasn't even true. Looking at her, I just wanted to shoot her in between her eyes, but I wasn't trying to end up back in jail.

"I'm so sorry, Jaxon." she said with tears streaming down her cheeks.

"Man save that shit. You knew exactly what you were doing when you did it. You know damn well you ain't sorry. You didn't even come see a nigga or even write me. You can save those bullshit ass tears you got going on too because they not making me feel bad for your ass at all."

"I really am sorry. It's just that I loved you so much back then, I felt like if I couldn't have you to myself, then nobody could. I wasn't thinking straight at all."

"Nope, you was letting another bitch think for you. But it's all good. I just know the next bitch that I get with won't be anything like you. I need me a bitch that knows how to talk about problems and shit. Not one that just assumes." She didn't say anything. She just sat there with a stupid look on her face. I needed me something to drink, and I was wondering why the hell our waiter hadn't come to our table yet? We had been sitting here for a little minute now.

"Where the hell is the waiter at?" I said more to myself than to Carla.

"I told them that we didn't need to be served because we weren't eating." Carla said.

"Why the fuck would you do some shit like that?"

"Because I had ate before I left the house." This bitch.

"So you just assume that I'm not hungry too huh? There you go with that shit. You only think about yourself. You need to get that shit together. I'm gonna let you know right now. Niggas don't like that assuming shit. You're not going to last in a relationship at all."

"That's the thing Jax. I don't want a relationship unless it's with you. You're the only man that I want. I still love you and I probably always will." I laughed in Carla's face.

"You love me? Nah, what you did damn sure wasn't love. You shady as fuck, Ma, and I can't fuck with it."

"But Jaxon…" I stopped her from finishing what she had to say by holding my hand up. I looked around and then signaled the waitress. She came over to the table with nothing but smiles. She was a pretty chick too. She was brown-skinned with a sexy ass short cut. Even though she was in her uniform, I could tell that she had a banging ass shape.

"How may I help you?" she asked smiling hard as hell. She even had pretty ass teeth. I couldn't help but smile back at her sexy ass.

"I'm sorry to bother you beautiful, but could you bring me a glass of water?" I asked. She blushed then her eyes shot over to Carla.

"Is that going to be all?"

"Yes." She smiled at me again and left our table, but not before giving Carla a dirty look. She probably thought Carla was my girlfriend, but I was going to let her know that I was single and ready to mingle.

"Really, Jaxon?" Carla asked. I looked at her and she had a look of disgust on her face.

"Really what?"

"Nigga, you know exactly what. You sat there and smiled all up in that hoe's face like I'm not sitting right here. That's so disrespectful." she said with an obvious attitude that I could care less about.

"It's not disrespectful to anyone because I'm not in a relationship. You mean nothing to me. So you need to get the hell on with that shit that you're talking." The pretty waitress came back and sat my glass on the table.

"Thank you, Michelle." I said reading her name tag. I was planning on getting her number before I left out of this bitch. "You done? You said all you needed to say?" I asked Carla once I drank all my water.

"So do you think that we can go back to how we used to be?"

"Hell no. You did some foul shit and now I'm done with you." I stood up from the table and threw a twenty down. I could tell by the look on Carla's face that she wanted to say more but she decided not to. I'm glad because I was beyond done with this conversation. It was obvious that something was seriously wrong with Carla because she really thought that I would take her back after all that she's done.

On my way out of the building, I ran into Michelle and got her number. She told me to call her later on tonight when she got off, but that wasn't all I planned on doing tonight either.

Chapter Ten

Alani

"You sure you're ready to do this?" Lena asked me as we pulled into a hotel parking lot.

"I'm more than ready." I let her know. We were now back in Miami, and I had business to handle. The first person on my list that I needed to see was Darius, and I was sure that I knew where he would be at too.

Lena and I got out of the car and went to go check in. I couldn't wait to see Darius. The best part of everything is, he's not even expecting me. This was going to be so great.

I had to leave Jacksonville. There was too much stuff going on. Legend stopped hitting me up, but I blame that on his stupid ass girlfriend. She was nothing but a hater. I wasn't tripping too much off of Legend because Juice would come whenever I called. It didn't matter what time of day it was. If I told him to come see me, he would drop everything. I didn't even care that he had a girlfriend, because she was the last thing on my mind when he was all up in my guts.

The last time he and I had sex, I realized that I had to leave. If I would've stayed, then I would've fallen in love with a man who has a girlfriend. His sex was just too damn good, and that shit was addicting. I didn't even have to dance at the club at all because this nigga would give me thousands of dollars every time we had sex.

He'd been calling and texting me since I'd gotten back to Miami earlier this morning, but I hadn't responded to anything. I left him in Jacksonville. Plus, he had a woman at home that he needs to be focused on. I'm leaving everything I did in Jacksonville, and I'm starting over again. Well, after I handle my business, then I'm starting over again.

"Bitch, I know you hear me talking to you." Lena said, pulling me out of my thoughts.

"What? I wasn't listening to your ass."

"I bet. Your hot ass probably over there thinking about Juice." I chuckled.

"Ain't nobody thinking about that nigga." She gave me a knowing look, because she knew that I was lying. I ignored her and went into the bathroom so that I could take a shower. I was happy as hell to be back in Miami. Only to get my revenge though. After I did what I needed to do, I was going to pay my brother a visit. I already knew he was probably losing his mind because he thought I was dead. I probably should've went to see him first, but I didn't want him to know what I had been through yet. He would try to go kill everyone himself and end up back in jail, and I wasn't having that shit.

"You ready?" I asked Lena after I was dressed. I had on a pair of black leggings and a black shirt. She looked at me like I was stupid.

"Bitch, why the fuck do you got on all black? The sun is still up, and it's like ninety degrees outside." she said laughing.

"Shut up. This is what I want to wear. Mind your business." I grabbed my purse and made sure I had my .45 in it. It wasn't going to be much talking when I saw Darius, but I did want him to see me though. I wanted to be the last person he saw before he took his last breath.

Pulling up to Darius and Jasmine's house, I got excited as hell. I was hoping like hell he was in here, but Darius wasn't the smartest person. Knowing him, he hadn't left the house since I killed Jasmine. I hope like hell his feelings were hurt when he came home and saw her dead body lying in front of the door. I looked over at Lena, and she was almost excited as I was. This was my bitch, for real. She knew exactly what I was planning to do and not once did she try to talk me out of it or tell me she wasn't helping me.

We stepped out of her car and casually walked up to the front door. Of course, this nigga had the door unlocked because he was a dumb ass. I chuckled at how stupid he was and walked into the house. The T.V downstairs was on but there was no one down here. Lena and I both had our guns drawn just in case he wasn't the only one in the house.

"I'm going to check the kitchen." I whispered to Lena. She nodded her head as I made my way into the kitchen. There wasn't anyone in there either. I was starting to get upset, because I felt like he wasn't in the house at all. I blew

87

out a frustrated breath and went to go find Lena so that we could go upstairs together. This bitch was standing in front of the T.V watching it.

"Bring yo ass." I told her. She turned around and looked at me like she wasn't sure if she wanted to come with me or not.

"I haven't seen this episode of Love and Hip Hop, though." she told me.

"You can watch it later. Come on." She reluctantly followed behind me as I went up the stairs. The master bedroom door was cracked, and I could hear someone in there snoring like a damn bear. I smiled to myself because I knew it was Darius.

I slowly pushed the door open and sure enough, this skinny ass nigga was knocked out on the bed.

"Eww, what the fuck done happened to this nigga?" Lena asked. She hadn't seen Darius in a long time. The last time she saw him, he was still good looking. Now he just looked like a crack head. I walked over to the bed and hit him in the face with the butt of my gun. His eyes shot open and his nose started bleeding.

"What the fuck?" he said sitting up. I aimed my gun at his head to make sure he didn't go anywhere.

"Hey Darius. Did you miss me?" I asked. His eyes widened as he looked at me. He looked like he had seen a ghost.

"Alani…What are you doing here?" he nervously asked.

"You didn't think you were going to stick your dirty ass dick inside of me every day and I was going to let you get away with it, did you? Come on, Darius. You're smarter than that."

"Let me explain. It was all Londyn's idea to kidnap you from the hospital." he said. I hit him again with my gun, and he screamed out in pain.

"Shut the fuck up, nigga. It was your idea to rape me every day. But it's okay. I'm here to handle you. You and Jasmine are going to be back together real soon." This nigga's eyes started watering, and I just laughed at him. I couldn't believe that once upon a time I had feelings for this nigga.

"Where's your phone at?" I asked. He grabbed it off the nightstand and tried to hand it to me.

"Nigga, I don't want it. Call Londyn and ask where she's at. If you do some funny shit, I'll blow your fucking brains out." He did what I told him to do and put it on speaker phone.

"What do you want, Darius?" Londyn asked once she answered the phone.

"Where you at?" he asked trying to sound normal as possible.

"Why the fuck you want to always know where I'm at? I already told you that I'm not fucking you no more." she snapped. I threw up a little bit in my mouth.

"Where are you? I might need a ride." he said.

"I'm at the mall with Los so I can't give you a ride anywhere. I'll see you later, though." she said, then hung up the phone. Of course she was with Los right now.

"Los has a new place." Darius let me know.

"Oh really? Do you know where it's at?"

"He lives in those condos by the mall, but I'm not sure which one he lives in." I nodded my head then shot Darius three times in the head. Blood and brain matter splattered all over the wall, and Lena and I hurried out of the house and back into her car.

"Damn bitch, it took you long enough. I was about to shoot the nigga myself." Lena said backing out of the driveway.

"Shut up. You wasn't about to do shit." I said. I wasn't really in a talking mood right now, because I was ready to put a couple of bullets in Londyn and Carlos. I was determined to find out which condo he stayed in, and I was going to sit my ass on that couch until they both walked through the door.

To my surprise, it wasn't hard to find his condo at all. His all-white Range Rover was parked right in front of it. I shook my head. They were making this way too easy for me.

"Pull in right here." I told Lena. She parked a couple cars down from his.

"Damn, this was too easy." Lena said, and I agreed with her.

"We're breaking in." I said.

"What? How?"

"Knowing Carlos, this is really the place he brings his bitches to fuck them. He doesn't care about this condo like he does that big ass estate he had us living in. I know for a fact that there's not an alarm or anything. He doesn't keep anything valuable here. So what I'm going to do is break the back window and then we're in." Lena looked like she didn't like my idea at all, but I didn't care. I was going to do this with or without her.

"Alright. Let's do it." We got out of the car and made our way to the back of the condo. Lena found a brick and handed it to me. I threw it as hard as I could into the window and it shattered. I was hype as hell as I climbed through the window.

There were pre-rolled blunts on the dresser, so I took one. We made our way to the living room, and I sat on the couch while Lena said she was going to hide out in the kitchen. I wasn't trying to hide at all. I wanted them both to see me. Now all that was left to do was wait. I lit my blunt and relaxed on the couch. I even put my feet up on the table with my gun resting on my lap.

I didn't even finish the whole blunt before the door opened and in walked Londyn and Carlos. It sounded like they were arguing as they made their way into the living room where I was still chilling and smoking my blunt.

"Damn, trouble in paradise?" I asked laughing. They both stopped in their tracks and looked at me. Londyn looked scared as hell while Carlos looked confused as hell.

"What the fuck?" Carlos said, trying to come towards me, but I shot him in the shoulder. He yelled out in pain as he fell to the ground. Londyn took off running out of the house as I sent two bullets her way. I missed and she got away, but Lena followed her. I stood up and walked over to where Carlos was laying on the floor. I couldn't deny the fact that he still looked good as hell. His hair had gotten longer. It came past his shoulders now. I just wanted to play all in it like I used to. I also wanted to take all of his clothes off and fuck him right here on the floor, but I couldn't. There was business that needed to be handled. He stood up and I had my gun trained on him aiming it directly at his head.

"Somebody playing games. How the fuck are you even here right now?" he had the nerve to ask.

"Because instead of killing me like a real nigga, you let them kidnap me. You should've got different people to hold me hostage. They didn't even tie me up or nothing." I laughed. He still had that confused look on his face.

"Man, what the fuck are you talking about?"

"Londyn and Darius. I know all about your little plan to kill my ass so that you and Londyn can live happily ever after. Well guess what. It didn't work." I smiled at him.

"Plan to kill you? You died in a car accident trying to get away from me. You died that same day. How the hell did I try to kill you? You know how devastated I was when that bitch ass doctor came out and told all of us that you were dead?" His eyes started watering and I started to feel different about this whole situation. Was this nigga lying about it because I'm still alive, or did he really not know that Londyn had kidnapped my ass? If he did know, he sure was doing some good ass acting.

"I didn't even know you were still alive. I didn't know that Londyn had kidnapped your ass. I would've been killed her and you know that." I could tell that he was mad as hell which only meant one thing. This nigga wasn't lying. He knew nothing about me still being alive. No wonder Londyn looked scared for her life then took off running. I dropped the gun on the floor and walked over to Carlos. Once I was close enough, he came and pulled me in for a hug. I didn't mean to start crying, but I couldn't stop the tears from falling even if I wanted to. I was about two seconds away from killing the man that I was very much still in love with. What if I would've just shot him without even talking first? He would be dead and I would've never known that this whole thing was really Londyn's fault. I was getting even more upset by just thinking about it. I hoped like hell that Lena caught her ass so I could end her life right here and right now.

"I'm sorry that I shot you." I said.

"It's all good. I'm just glad you didn't kill my ass." He kissed me all over my face, and I couldn't help but smile at

93

him. "I missed you so much." He said hugging me even tighter. Lena came back into the condo out of breath.

"That bitch was a fucking track star. I need some damn water." she said sitting down on the couch. I let Lena know everything wasn't Carlos' fault and she was glad.

"I didn't want to see you kill Carlos anyway. You know you still love that nigga." she said.

"We need to get to a hospital." I said when I saw all the blood that was covering Los' shoulder. I now felt bad as hell that I had shot him.

"I'm good. I just want to make sure you're alright." he told me. I looked up at him and something was different. His eyes were glossy as hell, and he looked like he hadn't been to sleep in a couple of days. It could've just been because he had just shed a couple of tears though. The sleepless nights could've came from missing me since he did think I was dead like everyone else. This shit was so crazy.

"I'm fine. Please just go to the hospital." I begged. He looked like he wanted to protest, but he finally agreed to go.

The whole ride to the hospital, I was silent. Carlos was trying to talk to me, but my mind was on Londyn. This crazy bitch had really kidnapped me just so she could be with Los and it worked. Well, it worked until my ass escaped. Darius was probably the one that helped her out because he was still salty that I didn't want his ass and that I shot him. I was glad that I killed him. I had no regrets after doing it either. I was going to sleep peacefully at night. Fuck Darius.

Next on my list was Londyn. Knowing her, she was probably trying to get out of town right now because she thought Carlos was coming for her. Little does she know that what I planned on doing to her was going to be much worse than whatever Carlos would do. I didn't even want him to help me out with killing her. The only thing I was going to need his help with was finding her for me. I knew for a fact that she wasn't stupid enough to stay in Miami after what she had done, but then again, she wasn't the brightest chick. I just hoped that wherever she was right now, she was enjoying herself because her days on this earth were numbered.

Chapter Eleven

Los

I didn't even want to be at the damn hospital because I already knew that the police was going to be all up in my business. I'd be damned if I told those pigs that Alani shot me. I had just gotten her back, and I didn't plan on losing her no time soon.

The bullet had went straight through, and I was glad. I couldn't even be mad at Alani for what she did, because I probably would've done the same thing if it was the other way around. I felt like less of a man though. This whole time, my girl wasn't dead. She was kidnapped by someone who I was with every day.

Londyn was there for me after Alani's funeral and everything, and the whole time she knew that she wasn't even dead. That's some straight psycho shit right there. She did the right thing by running though. If she would've stayed in that condo, then I probably would've killed her myself. I already knew that Alani was ready to kill her ass, but I didn't want Alani to do something that could put her behind bars for the rest of her life.

"Talk to me. You've barely said anything to me since we've been back." I said, laying down on the bed. We were back at the estate, and Alani had been quiet as hell since we had gotten back from the hospital.

"He raped me every day." she said barely above a whisper. I couldn't have heard her right.

"The fuck did you just say?" I asked louder than I intended to.

"Darius. He was raping me every day." I felt my blood start to boil after she repeated herself. I didn't even know what to say back to that. I got up off of the bed and walked over to the dresser so that I could get me some pills. I definitely needed to be high off of something stronger than weed to have this conversation with Alani. I popped two pills and sat back down on the bed.

"Isn't it too soon for you to be taking more pain meds?" she asked.

"None of that is important right now. Tell me everything that happened after that car accident." She lit the blunt that she was rolling and smoked it a little bit before she started talking.

"After the car accident, I remember waking up in a basement. That was the basement to Darius and Jasmine's house. I was still really sore, and I was still in that damn hospital gown. They weren't feeding me until Jasmine decided she wanted to be nice and help me out. She was bringing me food every day without them knowing." She took a shot of her Patron before she went on.

"Soon after that, he started raping me. It was every day with him. It's like he couldn't go a day without it. Londyn was also beating my ass every day, too. She would come in the basement and tell me stories about what y'all was doing and shit, and when I would say some smart shit, she would get mad and start beating my ass. Two months passed, and finally Jasmine helped me to escape. I had to kill her when I was leaving, though. I didn't trust that bitch."

"Kill her? What you mean you had to kill her?" I asked, shocked that she had just said that like killing someone was a normal everyday activity.

"I shot her ass in the head. Twice actually. I didn't know if she was just helping me because she actually felt bad for me, or if she was doing it for her own selfish reasons. Either way, I wasn't fucking with it and her ass had to go." I was at a loss for words. I always knew that Lani was a savage, but I never would've thought that she would actually kill someone.

"After that, I left Miami. I went to go find Lena. I knew she was in Jacksonville at her mom's house so that's where I went. I planned on getting myself together, then coming back to Miami so that I could kill you, Londyn, and Darius. I already killed Darius so now all that's left is Londyn. That bitch has another thing coming if she thinks she's gonna get away with what she did." Once again, I was shocked. Not only had she killed one person, she had killed two people. She was about to kill my ass and not lose an ounce of sleep over it. I was glad she wasn't the shoot first and ask questions last type. I would've been dead right now because she had honestly caught me slipping. As for Londyn, I wanted to kill her with my bare hands. I still couldn't believe that she did all of that just so she could be close to me again. She definitely needed to be taken care of.

Alani looked like she had gotten even more beautiful. I couldn't keep my damn eyes off of her. She looked up at me, then twisted her beautiful face up.

"Why are you just looking at me like that?" I asked.

"Because I can." I pulled her closer to me and kissed her. These last two months had been terrible without Alani. I wish I would've found out sooner that she was still alive because I definitely would have been searching high and low for her ass.

"I have to go see my brother tomorrow. I know he's not going to be too happy about this whole thing." she said. I watched as she finished off her blunt.

"I'll take you in the morning. I need to go see Ali anyway." I said. I needed to talk to him about this whole situation. I also needed to get back to work. I hadn't been myself, because Londyn had everybody thinking that Alani had died. I couldn't even focus on working. All I was doing was getting high, drunk, and fucking bitches. Being that she was never dead, I started to feel bad about what I had been doing with all of these other women. Technically it wasn't cheating because everyone thought Alani was dead right?

The next morning, I woke up refreshed as hell. This was the first night that I got through without having those nightmares of the day Alani had got into that accident. Knowing that Alani was indeed alive and not dead felt like a dream. Alani was knocked out beside me looking good enough to eat. Her burgundy hair looked good as hell on her. I still couldn't believe that she cut it. It didn't look bad or anything. I was just used to Alani having all of that hair that looked like weave.

I kissed her on her face, and she stirred in her sleep a little but didn't wake up. I threw the covers off of her and slapped her ass hard as hell. Her eyes flew open, and she started swinging at me. She hit me in my head real good, and I grabbed her arms. This was not the reaction that I was expecting.

"Alani! Chill! What the fuck you got going on?" I yelled. She calmed down and looked at me.

"I'm so sorry. I thought that I was back in that basement." she said out of breath. She looked so sad, and it made me even more upset that she had to go through that.

"You don't have to worry about them no more. I will take care of Londyn. Then you can sleep peacefully at night." I kissed her on her forehead then got up off of the bed. "Get dressed. We're going to Ali's crib." I told her. She sighed and slowly got off of the bed. Alani was not a morning person. I wouldn't be surprised if she had an attitude all morning. She'll be alright after she eats though. I just might take her ass to IHOP.

When we got to Ali's crib, I didn't know what to expect. Ever since Lena left him, he hadn't been the same. Yeah, he had been picking up my slack with the business and shit, but mentally, that nigga wasn't the same. I still couldn't even believe that he had another female in his house. The only girl he had ever brought to his house was Lena.

"Aye, fool!" I called out walking into the house. Of course this nigga's door wasn't locked. Alani sat down on the couch and started scrolling through her phone… probably talking to Lena. Ali came downstairs in nothing but his boxers, with his little bitch following right behind him like a damn lost puppy.

"Look at you out of the house before twelve." Ali joked. He went to go sit down on the couch and stopped when he saw Alani sitting there.

"Man, I know I'm not that damn high. Am I trippin' or does your new bitch look just like Alani?" he said. Alani looked up at him and laughed.

"Nigga it is me." she said getting up to give him a hug.

"How?" he turned to look at me. He had the same look on his face that I had when I saw Alani sitting on my couch.

"We'll talk about all of that later. We need to talk business right now." I let him know.

"Hi, I'm Draya. I didn't know that Carlos had a girlfriend." his little bitch said to Alani like she knew me personally and shit. She had her hand extended out and everything waiting for Alani to shake it. Alani looked at her then looked at her hand like it had a disease or something.

"What's up?" Alani asked, while looking back at her phone. Draya finally put her hand down when she realized that Alani wasn't going to shake it. I shook my head at Alani, but I knew she was only acting like that because of Lena.

I started walking towards the basement and Ali followed me. He had a blunt in his hand like always, and he looked like he was drunk, but maybe I was trippin'.

"So what the hell happened with Alani?" he asked sitting down on the couch.

"Man, Londyn kidnapped her and had everyone thinking that she was dead. She came to the crib yesterday trying to murk me and Londyn, because Londyn had put in her head that the whole kidnapping thing was my idea." I said shaking my head. I couldn't talk about this without getting mad. I reached into my pocket and pulled out two pills so that I could take them. Ali sat there with a shocked look on his face.

"Damn, that shit is crazy. Did y'all murk Londyn?" he asked.

"Man, hell nah. That bitch took off running as soon as she saw Alani. I'm pretty sure that she's not even in Miami no more. I'm gonna find her ass, though. And when I do, it's going to be lights out for her ass." I said meaning every word.

I walked over to the mini bar he had in his basement and opened up a bottle of Hennessy so I could pop these pills.

"Don't you think you need to slow down on the pills?" Ali asked, once I came to sit back down.

"Nah, I'm good. They help with the pain in my shoulder anyway. Alani shot my ass yesterday." I said, still not believing that shit happened. Ali started choking on the blunt he was smoking.

"I knew her ass was a savage." he said laughing.

"That shit ain't funny nigga. She was really trying to kill my ass. Her and Lena were just waiting on us when we got to the house."

"Lena? She's back in Miami?" Ali said, ignoring everything else that I had just said to him.

"Yeah. She came back with Alani." He just nodded his head probably thinking about looking for her. I was just hoping he didn't do anything stupid.

"But anyway, now that Alani is back, you going to be able to put in work now?" he asked, and I chuckled. It was beyond time for me to get back to work. I had been trippin' because I wasn't myself, but now that I had my girl back, I had to get back to the money.

"Yeah, it's time to get back to the money." I said, resting my head on the couch. I was high as hell from the pills that I had just taken. I wasn't even taking the pills that the doctor prescribed me. The ones that I'd been taking made me numb to everything. That's why I was still taking them. After my shoulder healed, I planned on not taking them anymore. I knew that Alani wouldn't be too happy if she knew that I was popping pills and shit. She thought that I was taking the pills that I was prescribed but I wasn't.

"Good, it's a nigga named Legend that wants to get on with us. That nigga said he just moved down here from Jacksonville with his lady, and he needs to make some fast money. I told him that I had to run it by you first before I let him know anything." Ali told me handing me the blunt. I was already high as fuck so I didn't need to be smoking, but I took it anyway.

"Shit, if he seems like he ain't on no snake shit then put him on. But if he is, put a bullet through that nigga's skull." Ali looked at me like I had lost my mind.

"You sure?"

"Hell yeah."

"You don't even want to meet the nigga first?"

"Nah, I'm good." I said, inhaling the smoke from the blunt. I guess I should've met the nigga myself so that I could see if he was a snake or not, but my girl was home. I planned on marrying her ass as soon as I could, then filling her ass up with all of my kids. Speaking of kids, I needed to get Jr. from Tammy's mom.

After Tammy was killed, I wasn't in the right mind to care for a child by myself. I had always pictured Lala and I raising kids together, but shit wasn't going how I planned. Shit, me and her hadn't even talked about that whole situation with my son. I didn't know how she was feeling about it., but however she was feeling, I was going to need her to be on board, because I planned on raising my son in my house. Shit was about to be different, but I knew me and her would get through it.

Chapter Twelve

Lena

I had to admit, it felt real good being back in Miami. Jacksonville was just too boring for me. I guess it was boring because I was starting to miss my old life, but who was I kidding? I missed Ali. I missed the hell out of that nigga. I really wanted to go see him and we patch everything up, but I also didn't want to be that girl who kept taking her cheating ass nigga back. He really did break my heart, because I had plans on marrying this nigga and he did this to me.

I couldn't help but feel like I wasn't good enough for him. I did everything that I was supposed to do. I didn't even look at another nigga while Ali and I were together. I quit stripping and everything when we were together. Just for him. I made sure I sucked him dry every single night, and that still wasn't enough for him. He still wanted more.

"Lena, are you listening to me?" Leslie asked, pulling me out of my thoughts that I was having about Ali.

"I'm sorry, what did you say?" I asked.

"I said that Legend called me Alani last night when we were fucking." I was shocked. I didn't even know what to say back to her.

"Damn, for real? That's so fucked up."

"I hate that bitch. If she would've just kept her legs closed, I wouldn't even be going through any of this. He was fucking that hoe in our house, Lena. Our house. He could've at least took her to a hotel or some shit." Leslie and Legend had moved down here from Jacksonville a few days ago, and she wanted to meet up with me so that we could talk. She didn't have any friends here yet, so I said why not chill with her a little bit? Right now, we were at Red Robbin because that's where she said she wanted to eat.

"Look Leslie, me and you are cool and all, but I'm not about to sit here and let you call Alani all types of bitches and hoes. I understand that you're upset that Legend cheated on you or whatever, but you can't just blame her. Like I said, he was the one pushing all up on her at the mall, so if anybody's a hoe, it's your cheating ass nigga." I let her know. I wasn't feeling how she was just sitting here talking shit about Alani like she was a big ass hoe or some shit.

"Why did she have to go after my man, though? Why can't she get her own?" she asked looking sad as hell.

"She does have her own. She's with Los. They were just going through some things when we were in Jacksonville, but they're good now." I said, pulling my phone out of my purse to see if I had any missed calls or text messages.

"Los? She's back with Los?" Leslie said with nothing but hatred in her eyes.

"Yes. That's her fiancé." I said. Leslie looked even more upset. She looked as if she was going to break down crying right here. I didn't know what all that was about, but I didn't even ask her. I had a two missed calls from Alani and a text message.

Lani: Bitchhhh Ali got some hoe living up in y'all house!

I don't know why, but I felt my heart drop to the pit of my stomach. I don't know why I thought Ali wouldn't move on. Shit, I wasn't even in Miami anymore, and I changed my number so that he couldn't try to talk to me.

I heard a familiar voice so I looked up from my phone. I thought my eyes were playing tricks on me when I saw my cousin Draya walking towards us holding hands with Ali. *What the hell?* I was staring a hole through Draya as she smiled like she had just hit the lottery. She finally looked at me and wore a smirk on her face that I wanted to slap off.

"Hey Lenaaaa." she sang making her way over to our table. I didn't say anything. I just looked at her grimy ass. She knew all about Ali. She knew that he was my nigga, she knew that he had cheated on me, and she knew that I left Miami because of him. She couldn't wait to get me out of the picture so she could slide her hoe ass right in.

Ali looked at me then he quickly let her hand go and stepped away from her. It was too late. I had already seen them acting like they were the world's happiest couple. I couldn't do anything but shake my head. I wanted to cry, but at the same time, I wanted to beat this bitch's ass. I wanted to drag her out of this establishment by the ugly, cheap ass weave that she had in her head.

"When did you get back in town? I heard you were in Jacksonville." she said. I closed my eyes hoping to calm myself down, because right now, the only way I was going to get out of here was in handcuffs.

"Oh, this is my boyfriend Ali. Ali, this is my cousin Lena." she smiled. Ali looked at her like he wanted to strangle her stupid ass. I felt the same exact way.

"Bitch, you got a lot of nerve." I finally said chuckling.

"What?" she had the nerve to have a shocked look on her face. She knew exactly what I was talking about.

"So, those nights I called you crying about Ali and how he wasn't shit just went in one ear and out the other, huh? Bitch, you knew that was my nigga. You are friends with him on Facebook! You used to comment on our pictures." I stopped talking and just started laughing. I really needed to get out of here because I was really two seconds away from putting my hands on her.

"Girl, get out your feelings. Ali was single since you wanted to run from your problems, and now he's mine." she said. Before she could even react, I picked up the glass that I was drinking out of and smashed it in her face. She screamed and fell to the ground. After that, I grabbed her by her weave and started punching her in the face. I continued to punch her until I blacked out.

The last thing I remember is Ali pulling me off of Draya and yelling at me about the police coming and shit. When I realized it was him who grabbed me, I quickly snatched away from him and stormed off. I didn't want that nigga touching me at all. I didn't even want to be around him. I was so mad that he was with Draya, and I felt my eyes watering up, but I didn't dare let a tear fall from my eyes. I was not about to sit here and cry over Ali. It's just a matter of time before he cheats on her ass, too. And she is going to deserve that shit.

I jumped in my car and sped out of the parking lot. I needed to see Alani. I turned the radio all the way up and sped through traffic. That's when the gas light came on and I remembered that I told myself that I was going to get gas after I left from Red Robbin with Leslie. I rolled my eyes and headed to the nearest gas station.

"Can I get twenty on pump two please?" I said to the cashier at the register.

I started to hand her the twenty dollar bill that was in my hand when a familiar voice said from behind me, "I got it."

I turned around to be face to face with Jaxon's fine ass. He was looking even better than the last time I had seen him. He was wearing Gucci from head to toe, his hair was still in a curly fro with tapered sides, and his Versace cologne filled my nostrils making me wet as hell.

"No… It's okay. You don't have to." I told him. He looked at me and chuckled.

"I already did, Ma. You were too busy raping a nigga with your eyes to notice." He smiled at me showing his perfect white teeth. His hazel eyes were piercing through my soul. I wanted to jump on him right here, and I didn't care who watched. I had to look away from him.

"Thanks for paying for my gas." I said then hurried out of the store. Why was Jax so damn fine? Why was he making me feel like a little nervous school girl when he was in my presence? I couldn't even pump my gas in peace. When I looked up, there his fine ass was making his way over to me.

"Aye, I've been wanting to talk to you. You should give me your number so that I can hit you up later." he said. As much as I wanted to say no, I couldn't. He was looking way too good for me to turn him down. He handed me his phone, and I quickly put my number in it. He smiled at me and told me that he would hit me up later. I watched as he walked to his car, and I just shook my head when I saw a female sitting on the passenger's side. This nigga was all in my face but had a whole bitch waiting in the car for him. Niggas ain't shit, I swear.

I got back in my car and headed towards Carlos and Alani's house. They were letting me stay with them until I found my own place. Their house was so damn big, they wouldn't even know that I was there anyway.

When I got to the estate, Alani was at the kitchen table drinking Remy straight from the bottle. I really wished she would stop with the drinking, but she kept telling me that she didn't have a problem, but I didn't believe that one bit. She didn't even eat breakfast before she started drinking. I went over to the table and sat down in front of her.

"Hey girl, why you looking soooo down?" Alani slurred. I could tell she was drunk as hell. I didn't even want to tell her what had happened today with Ali, because she probably wouldn't even remember the conversation.

"Have you talked to Jaxon yet?" I asked. She looked at me and rolled her eyes.

"No, I haven't talked to him. He hasn't tried to talk to me eitherrrrr." she said.

"Alani, he still thinks you're dead. You know how your brother feels about you. You need to talk to him. Let him know everything that's happened." I said. She started giggling like what I had said was a joke. I just shook my head at her. She lit the blunt that had been sitting on the table and closed her eyes as she inhaled it.

"I wish I was really dead." she said. She was really trippin' right now.

"Alani…" I started to say but she cut me off.

"I want to be dead, Lena! Carlos won't even touch me anymore! That nigga's sex drive is high as hell, and he won't touch me. I already know he's fucking other bitches. I can feel that shit. I never should've told him that I was raped. Then maybe he wouldn't look at me as damaged goods." she said sadly. Her eyes started watering up and a tear fell down her cheek. She quickly wiped it away and took another shot of Remy.

"Alani, Carlos doesn't look at you as damaged goods. He loves you more than life itself." I tried to tell her.

"No he doesn't. If he loved me, then he would be here with me right now. He hasn't answered not one of my phone calls. He just dropped me off and left without saying shit to me. I'm not stupid, Lena. His phone kept ringing but he wouldn't answer it. He kept sending whoever was calling to voicemail." I knew exactly how Alani was feeling. I went through the same thing. I just hoped like hell that Carlos got his shit together, because I didn't like seeing my best friend like this.

I sat with Alani trying to comfort her for two hours, then she finally decided that she wanted to go to bed, and I was right behind her. I would just have to wait until the morning time to talk about what happened today with Draya and Ali. I didn't get to see her face after I finished beating her ass, but I was hoping that I made her cute little face look ugly as hell.

I got into bed and snuggled up under the covers. I was glad that Ali didn't have my number or anything, because I already knew that he would've been blowing me up right now. After today, I really didn't want anything to do with him. I was going to keep him where he belonged and that was in the past.

As soon as I closed my eyes and got comfortable, my phone started ringing.

"Hello?" I said obviously annoyed.

"What's good, Ma? It's Jaxon."

Chapter Thirteen

Ali

I couldn't even believe what had happened between Lena and Draya. I left the house with intentions of eating good as hell and Draya insisted on going. She should've stayed her ass at the house, but she always wanted to be seen with me to make girls think she was my girlfriend. I didn't know what to think when I saw Lena sitting there looking like the goddess that she was. Even without trying, Lena was still the most beautiful girl in the whole establishment. Draya couldn't touch Lena even on her best day.

Finding out that Draya and Lena were cousins was a shocker. What was even more shocking was that Draya knew that Lena and I used to be together and she didn't even care. That's some grimy shit right there. That's just some shit you don't do to family. That's why when Lena started beating her ass, I didn't even try to stop her. Draya was getting everything she deserved. Had I known that they were family, I wouldn't have given her the time of day.

If it wasn't for the girl that Lena was with yelling at me to do something, Draya might have been dead by the hands of Lena. I have to admit that seeing Lena beating Draya's ass like that had my dick hard as hell. I knew Lena wasn't fucking with me anymore by the look she gave me when I tried to pull her off of Draya, and that shit fucked with me, too. I had to get Lena back. She was going to be my wife. She just didn't know it yet.

"Look at my fucking face! I'm pressing charges on that bitch!" Draya yelled while looking at herself in the bathroom mirror. I was sitting on the bed smoking a blunt, and of course, thinking about Lena. Draya had been bitching about what happened the whole way home like it wasn't her fault. She really started all of this and was mad because she got her ass beat.

"Look at my eye, Ali! Do you see this shit? My eye has never been swollen like this or even black. I've never had a black eye! And you just let the bitch jump on me!" she yelled some more. I was getting tired of hearing her talk about this shit like it wasn't her fault.

"Stop calling her a bitch, man." I said. I didn't like how she was just disrespecting Lena like that.

"Are you serious? She just beat my ass, and all you're worried about is me calling her a bitch?" she yelled in disbelief.

"If you wouldn't have walked your stupid ass over to their table, then you wouldn't have gotten your ass beat. You can't be mad at no one but yourself. You knew what you were doing." I said turning on the T.V.

"Wow, really? You think this is my fault? Is that why it took you so long to pull that hoe off of me?" she asked coming over to my side of the bed.

"Hell, yeah. You and her are cousins, and you knew all about who I was before I even met you. That's grimy as fuck and you know it. You deserved that ass whoopin." I let her know. She just looked at me like she wanted to hit me, but she knew better than to try it. Her face was fucked up though. Her right eye was swollen shut, she had a big gash on her forehead, she had cuts and bruises all over her cheeks, and underneath her other eye was a big ass purple bruise. Lena had really fucked her up.

"You ain't no better than me, Ali. You still got me up in your house right?" She said smirking. She was right though. If I was trying to get Lena back, I was probably going to need to stop fucking with her cousin, but it's not my fault that I didn't know. Draya did this shit on purpose. To be honest, I felt like this bitch had been doing nothing but using me.

"You right. Get the fuck out." I calmly said. She looked at me with her mouth hanging open. Her lip was busted, too. She was just looking really bad.

"Are you serious?"

"As a heart attack. You didn't do shit but use me anyway, so call you an Uber or some shit, and get the fuck out." I said finishing off the blunt that I was smoking.

"I didn't use you! I love you, Ali. I thought you felt the same way about me." she said, with tears running down her face.

"And that's what you get for thinking. Why y'all females always do that? Why can't y'all just fuck and let it be just that?"

"Nigga, you moved me into your house! You're always paying for me to get my hair done! You even take me shopping! You lead me on thinking we were something that we're not." I chuckled at how mad she was. The only woman I would ever love is Lena.

"You right shawty. I shouldn't have done none of that. I didn't tell you to quit your job, though, so that one was on you. It's your fault that you don't have money anymore. You're not my woman though. You were just a bitch that I was fucking. And if Lena ever decides she wants to take me back, she's coming back with no problems. At the end of the day, it's always going to be her." She didn't say anything. She just looked at me and cried. I didn't care about none of this shit. I needed to get my shit together and get my woman back. Draya was nothing but a distraction.

"You ain't shit." she said grabbing her phone then storming out of the room. I didn't have to worry about Draya trying to destroy my shit. She wasn't about that life like Lena was. I needed to talk to Alani, though. I knew that she knew where Lena was, and hopefully, she wouldn't be difficult and would just tell me where she was at.

The next morning, I woke up and took a quick shower. I had plans to go over to Los' crib and see what was up with

Alani. She seemed different the last time I saw her, but maybe that was just me trippin'.

I didn't even tell Los that I was on the way to his crib, but most of the time, I never did anyway. The only thing that was on my mind was Lena. I wondered if she found anybody else. The thought of her fucking another nigga had me mad as fuck. I couldn't be mad at no one but myself though, because I was the one that was fucking her cousin. I really didn't know what the hell I was thinking when I cheated on Lena, but that was a mistake that I was not trying to make ever again.

I pulled up to Los' crib and jumped out of my car. I hated these damn security guards. They always searched me like they didn't know that Los and I were cousins. I told him about that shit, but he always says, "You can never have too much protection." I feel that shit, but damn. These nigga's really be doing too much.

After they were done searching me, I made my way into the house. I was happy as hell when I saw Alani sitting at the table. She had an empty bottle of Patron sitting in front of her and she was struggling trying to roll a blunt.

"Lani." I said getting her attention. She looked up at me and rolled her eyes. I could tell that she had been crying cause her eyes were red and puffy as shit.

"What?" she said with an attitude. I didn't understand why she had an attitude with me. I hadn't done shit to her ass.

"Where's Los?"

"He said he was handling business with you, so I don't know where the hell that lying ass nigga is at." She got up, went to the refrigerator, and pulled out another bottle of Patron.

"He said he was with me? I haven't talked to that nigga since yesterday." I said more to myself but she heard me anyway. She scoffed and sat back down at the table. I was going to have to see what was up with Los, too, because he was really being messy with his shit right now.

"Have you seen Lena?" I asked. Before Alani could answer, Lena walked into the kitchen with her phone glued to her ear smiling hard as hell, and I instantly got heated. Who the fuck was she talking to this early, and why was she smiling so damn hard? She walked right passed me and went to the refrigerator to get out a bottle of water.

"Boy, you so crazy." she said, then started laughing. I bit the inside of my jaw trying not to snatch her phone from her and throw it against the wall.

"Lena, lemme holla at you real quick." I said. She looked at me, rolled her eyes, and kept it moving like I didn't say anything to her. I followed right behind her because she had me fucked up if she thought she was just going to walk right past me like I wasn't talking to her.

"Let me call you back." she said to whoever she was on the phone with. She turned to face me with a scowl on her face and her arms folded.

"Nigga, me and you don't got shit to talk about. Go talk to Draya. That is your girlfriend right?" she spat.

"No that girl ain't my girlfriend. The only girl I want is standing right in front of me." she chuckled and rolled her eyes again.

"That's not your girlfriend, but she's living up in your house. The house that you had me living in. Do you move all of your bitches in that house? Is that why that white bitch felt the need to just pop up because she lived there at one point, too?"

"No Lena…" I said but she cut me off.

"Fuck you, nigga. We don't have anything to talk about. I wish you and Draya the best though because I'm done. I don't need people like you in my life anyway." she said. She turned and walked up the circular staircase and disappeared into her room. I felt defeated. I don't know why I thought Lena would just take me back like I didn't do some foul shit, but I wasn't going to stop until she was mine again.

Los walked through the front door, and this nigga looked high as hell. I knew he was addicted to pill; I watched how he started to act after the whole Alani thing had happened. He looked at Alani who was drinking the bottle of Patron like it was water and didn't say shit to her. He just walked right over to me.

"What's good, fool? What you doing here?" he slurred. This nigga was fucked up.

"Aye bruh, I need to talk to you." I let him know.

"Oh aight." he said, walking up the stairs and heading in the direction of the conference room. He closed the door behind him and sat down at the table.

"What you on, Los?" I asked getting right to the point. He looked at me like he was confused.

"What you talkin' about nigga?"

"Where you coming from?"

"I went to see my son." he said, but I didn't believe that shit at all.

"Nigga, it's lipstick and shit on your shirt. You got a big ass hickey on your neck. What bitch you fucking? Don't even try to lie and say it's Alani, because you told her that you was with me earlier when you know damn well you wasn't."

"I did go see my son. Tammy's mom Janelle was looking good as hell too, so I had to get a little sample." I couldn't even say nothing to this nigga. He was really fucking his baby mom's mother. What kind of shit was that? I just shook my head at him.

"You need to get your shit together, bruh." I said. He waved me off like what I was saying wasn't the truth.

"Nigga, I know what I'm doing."

"I said the same thing. And now look. Lena doesn't want nothing to do with me. I don't want you to end up like me because Alani is a good girl. You see how hurt you was when you thought she was dead. You're going to feel even worse if you get caught and she leaves your ass." I said standing up. I didn't have time to be sitting here and lecturing this grown ass man. At the end of the day, he was going to do what he wanted anyway, so what I was saying was basically pointless.

The only thing I was really worried about was getting Lena back. All this other shit was irrelevant.

Chapter Fourteen

Alani

Looking at Carlos right now was making me sick to my stomach. I really wanted to just punch him in his lying ass face, but I was gonna let him live. For now anyway. This nigga was cheating on me, and I knew it. At first, I could feel it. He wouldn't touch me at all, but now he's lying about where he's going and where he's been. He's sending me straight to voicemail when I call him, and he was now letting the sun beat him home. I didn't like this shit at all.

You would think that all that I've been through, he would be there for me, trying to comfort me and shit, but nope. This nigga is too busy thinking with his dick. I didn't know what it was that I wanted to do. I didn't want to stay and be that weak ass bitch that stays with her boyfriend knowing he was cheating. I also didn't want to leave him because I really did love him. I've never loved a man as much as I loved him, and it was breaking my heart that he was cheating on me with other bitches.

"Where were you at?" I asked sitting on the bed with my arms folded. He looked at me with those glossy ass eyes and acted like I didn't say shit to him. He went right into the bathroom and got in the shower. Of course. I didn't even want to be in the same house as Carlos right now. I decided that I was going to finally go see my brother. I know he was going to be feeling some type of way when he saw me, but I was just gonna have to deal with it.

I got out of the bed and slid on some sweatpants and a tee shirt. I ran my fingers through my hair then hurried downstairs and out of the house. I didn't want Carlos to see me leaving at all. I even left my phone on the dresser just because I wanted him to worry about me. I grabbed his keys off of the counter and was out of the door. Fuck him.

When I pulled up to Jaxon's house, I got nervous. I didn't know why he wasn't the first person I came to see when I first got back in Miami. I just hoped that he wouldn't be too upset with me.

I got out of the car and walked up to the front door. To my surprise, the door was unlocked. I couldn't believe it. All the lights were off as I stepped into the house. It was nice as hell in there and clean. It was 12:00 AM so I didn't know if Jaxon was sleeping or not.

Making my way up the stairs, I could hear talking. There was only one room with a light on so I figured that was the room he was in. I took a deep breath before walking into his room, and boy was I in the shock of my life.

Lena was riding him reverse cowgirl with her eyes closed. What the hell was Lena doing over here anyway? No, a better question is why the hell was she fucking my brother?

"What the fuck?" I said loud enough for them to hear me. Lena's eyes flew open and she looked at me.

128

"Alani, oh my goodness!" she said getting off of Jax and trying to cover herself up.

"Alani?" Jax said sitting up on the bed and looking at me. He looked from me to Lena then got off the bed and put on a pair of basketball shorts. I was glad that he did that because I really didn't think I would've been able to have this conversation while he was naked.

"Alani, don't get mad." Lena said with the covers covering her up.

"Mad at what?" I asked confused.

"Wait, somebody better start explaining shit to me before I get mad." Jaxon said. The look on his face let me know that he was already mad. I didn't blame him at all though. I sat down on the bed and told him everything that had happened since the car accident. I could tell that he wanted to find Londyn and kill her himself.

"So why didn't you let me know you were still alive when you first got back to Miami?" he asked.

"I've been dealing with some personal issues, Jax. You wouldn't understand." I let him know. I really didn't think that he would understand. I got raped every day for two months straight by a man that I used to love. I don't care what anyone says; that's just not something that you get over the next day. Then, Los isn't making it no better because he wouldn't even comfort me. He was too damn busy thinking about other bitches to worry about me. I shook my head just thinking about it.

"You know what, I'm not even mad at you. Just don't do no stupid shit like this again." he said hugging me. I couldn't even enjoy the hug because this nigga was all sweaty and shit. Images of him and Lena having sex flashed through my head, and I quickly broke from his embrace. This was something that I was going to have to get used to, but it's weird as hell to me. Lena and Jaxon? I didn't even know that they had a thing for each other.

"Well, I'll let y'all finish. I'll be downstairs if you guys need me." I said getting up to leave the room. I was heading right downstairs to see what Jax had to drink. I was now wishing that I had my phone with me because I was about to be bored as hell, but I was also hoping that Carlos was losing his mind wondering where I was at just like I'd been doing with him lately.

I was glad to see that Jaxon had plenty to drink. I wanted to be fucked up, so I grabbed the bottle of Hennessy and a shot glass and made my way to the couch. I turned on the T.V. not really caring about what I was watching, I just wanted some sound. I didn't have anything to smoke, but I was sure Jaxon did. He was a real pot head. I would just have to wait until him and Lena were finished handling their business.

Before I had even realized it, I had drunk half the bottle. I didn't think I was drunk until I stood up to go use the bathroom, and I could barely keep myself up.

"Damn, Alani. Can you go one day without drinking?" Lena asked helping me into the bathroom. She was always so worried about me and my drinking. I wasn't harming anyone, so why was it bothering her so much? I looked at her and started laughing. I didn't know what the hell I was laughing at, but I was laughing like she had just told the funniest joke.

There was loud knocking coming from the front door and Jaxon came downstairs with his gun in his hand. It was late as hell, so who the fuck was banging on his door like that?

"Alani! Open up this fucking door before I shoot this bitch down!" Carlos yelled from the other side of the door. I rolled my eyes and made my way to the door. *How the hell did this nigga find me?* I thought to myself. I stumbled to the door and opened it. Carlos had murder in his eyes and I didn't understand why.

"What nigga you got up in here?" he asked jacking me up by my shirt.

"Me, nigga." Jaxon said from behind us. He was still standing there with his gun in his hand ready for whatever. I didn't like how this was going at all. Carlos looked at Jaxon like he wanted to end his life right then and there, but he didn't. He just pushed me out of the house and told me to get in the car. I didn't want to, but I didn't want my brother and Los getting into it because of me either.

I slowly walked over to the passenger's side of the car and got in. He grilled Jaxon the whole way until he got into the driver's seat.

"What the fuck is wrong with you, Alani?" Carlos yelled.

"No nigga, what the fuck is wrong with you?" I shot back.

"Why the fuck would you just leave the house like that without telling me where you were going? Did you really think you were gonna take my car, and I wasn't gonna find yo' ass?! I got a tracking device on every single one of my cars!" He yelled. Damn, I needed to get my own car then. This nigga really can track his own cars.

"You always leave without telling me where you're going! Then, when you do tell me where you're going, you're lying about it because you ain't shit but a lying ass nigga!" He looked at me and I could tell that he was trying to calm himself down by the way he was biting the insides of his cheek.

"You trippin' Alani. Ain't nobody been lying to you."

"Nigga, you came home with a hickey on your damn neck! I'm not stupid!" He ignored me like I didn't say anything to him. He had been doing that a lot now lately. I wanted to cry, but what for? It seems like every nigga I get with cheats on me like I'm nothing. I could leave Los whenever I wanted to, but I didn't want to do that. I loved that man with all my heart, and I wanted to become his wife. I looked down at my finger and saw the engagement ring that I had yet to take off. I didn't even take it off when I was in

Jacksonville fucking with Juice and Legend. I guess I just wasn't ready for it to truly be over between the two of us.

I really just wanted to know who this bitch was that he was spending so much of his time with. What made her so special? Why did he feel the need to cheat on me with her? What did this bitch look like? Shit, she better look better than me or it's going to be a serious problem. I needed to know the answer to all of these questions and I was going to. I wanted to see for myself firsthand what this nigga was doing. I don't know how I would react to seeing Carlos actually cheating on me, but something had to be done. This nigga really thought that it was okay to cheat on me like I was trash or some shit. That shit wasn't about to go down like that though. He had me so fucked up, and I couldn't wait to rain on his little parade.

When we got back to the house, I didn't say shit to him. I didn't have shit to say to him. He came to Jax's house acting a complete fool when he was out here doing God knows what. I got in bed and turned my back towards him. He didn't even try to talk to me either. This nigga had the nerve to do the same thing to me. He was acting like I had done something wrong in this situation, when I hadn't done anything at all. I couldn't believe it. I pushed everything that happened today to the back of my head and closed my eyes. Soon enough, I drifted off to sleep.

Waking up alone in bed didn't shock me at all. I wouldn't be shocked if Los wasn't even here right now. Shit, he was probably at his other chick's house. The thought alone had me ready to hunt him down and shoot him in the face for playing with my feelings like this. Who the hell did he think he was?

I sat up in bed and threw the covers off of me. I needed to drink. I didn't even care about eating breakfast knowing I shouldn't be drinking on an empty stomach. I really needed to figure out what I was going to do because I wasn't about to sit here and let him cheat on me like it's okay. He needs to know that I'm not about to take this bullshit at all. I don't care how much I love him. The old Alani would stay and pretend that everything is all good, but not the new Alani. I've gotten fucked over too many times in the past and I'm sick of it.

I was debating on what it is I should drink and Los walked through the door. He came into the kitchen and stood behind me, but I ignored him. I didn't have shit to say to him, because I knew he had probably just come from being with that bitch. I needed something strong, so I grabbed the bottle of Hennessy. I took a shot straight from the bottle and walked past him so that I could sit on the couch.

"You didn't cook breakfast?" he had the nerve to ask. I chuckled and took another shot. Why didn't he eat when he was at his other girl's house? He came into the living room and stood in front of me. He didn't look like himself at all. Like always, his eyes were glossy and they were bloodshot red. His hair was all over the place, and he looked tired as hell.

Looking into his eyes, I could see that this wasn't the man that I had fallen in love with. This was an asshole that I was just living with. He was high on something that wasn't just weed. I could tell.

"You don't hear me talking to you?" he asked looking at me with anger written all over his face.

"If you're so hungry, go in the kitchen and fix you something to eat. I don't know why you didn't eat while you were at that bitch's house anyway." I said rolling my eyes and taking another shot. His crazy ass stared at me for a good five minutes. Out of nowhere, he started laughing. What the hell was he laughing at? I didn't say anything that was meant to be funny.

"Alani, get your ass up and go cook some damn breakfast. I'm hungry as hell. And hurry the fuck up. I got business to handle." he said. I looked at him like he was crazy. He definitely wasn't talking to me like this.

"Fuck you and that *business* you got to handle!" I yelled feeling myself getting even more upset. The next thing I knew, Carlos backhanded me hard as hell and made me fall off of the couch. I dropped the bottle, and it was spilling all over the floor.

"Who the fuck you think you're talking to?!" he yelled. I didn't know what to do so I just laid there on the floor. My face stung from the powerful slap he delivered to my face. Did he really just put his hands on me? I sat up and looked up at him. Tears stung my eyes, but I wouldn't dare let them fall.

He looked like a madman. He looked as if he was ready to end my life and dump me in the river.

"When I tell you to do something, that means do it." he said looking down at me like I was disgusting him. I didn't say anything to him though. What could I say? He was really on one right now. I got up and went back into the bedroom. This was it for me. I couldn't stay here with this man. I know for a fact that he is cheating on me, but putting his hands on me is where I have to draw the line. No man should ever put his hands on the woman he claims he loves. That's just something that should never happen.

I sat down on the bed thinking about how Los and I used to be. Everything between us used to be so simple. There was a time when Los would try to kill a nigga for staring at me for too long. I remember when he couldn't wait to come home to me after being gone all day making us money. Then, there was a time when he wanted me to have all twenty of his kids. I wasn't trying to hear that though so he went and had a baby by someone else. I shook my head at the thoughts that I was having. I was still in shock that he had really put his hands on me.

"Alani," Carlos said standing in the door. "I don't know what happened down there. I lost control of myself. I should've never put my hands on you." he said. I just looked at him. So now he wanted to have some love and compassion? Just a few minutes ago, he was ready to kill me because I didn't want to cook breakfast. He didn't look like a madman anymore. He almost looked like himself, but his eyes were still glossy.

He walked closer to me and pulled me in for a hug. He kept telling me how sorry he was, but it was too late for apologies. He couldn't take back what he had just done. I knew that after this, Los and I would never be the same. He hugged me for a good five minutes before he finally pulled away. He looked like he actually cared about how I was feeling for once.

"I'll be back. I gotta go handle some business." he said. Of course he had to go handle some business. I feel like that's every nigga's excuse for when they're about to go cheat on you. I didn't even say anything back. He kissed me on my forehead, and I just watched him as he left out of the room.

As soon as he left, I grabbed my duffle bag and started packing my clothes. I was leaving, because there was no way that I could stay here with Carlos right now. Yeah, he apologized for putting his hands on me, but apologies don't fix everything. If I stayed, Los would think it was okay to hit me, and I would probably become his punching bag.

I think time apart from each other is for the best. We both need to get ourselves together. I know what I want. I still want him. I still want to marry him and even have his kids one day, but as of right now, I just don't see that happening.

After I was finished packing my things, I called Lena so that she could come get me. I was going to be staying with Jaxon until I got my own spot. I already had it planned out that I was going to try to get a job so I wouldn't run out of the money that I still had left over.

I felt bad about just leaving Los without letting him know why I was leaving so I made sure to leave him a letter. After I had finished writing the letter, I took my engagement ring off and sat it beside of the letter on the dresser. As soon as I was finished, Lena texted me and let me know that she was outside. This was the hardest thing I think I've ever had to do, but it had to be done.

I gathered all of my belongings and made my way downstairs. I took one last look around before leaving out of the house. This would probably be the last time that I would be in here and it made me sad. I had grown to love this estate just as much as I loved Los. I shook my head and left out of the front door. Hopefully, Carlos would realize what he had and get himself together real soon.

Chapter Fifteen

Los

I was fucked up about how I had put my hands on Alani like that. I was on some other shit for real, but it was the pills that make me act that way. I was addicted to them shits too. I was ashamed to let anyone know because I didn't want them judging a nigga or anything, and I was hoping that I could just stop without needing any professional help.

After I left the house, I headed straight over to Janelle's crib. Janelle was Tammy's mom. She was keeping Jr. for me, and I would come over every day so I could see him. I didn't mean to start fucking Janelle, but I just couldn't help it. She was bad as hell to be thirty-five, and she had Tammy when she was young as hell, but you couldn't even tell that she had any kids.

Janelle didn't look her age at all, and if I didn't know her, I would think that she was in her mid-twenties. She and Tammy looked like they could be twins really. The only difference was that Janelle's skin was light as hell, and Tammy had chocolate skin. I guess she got that from her dad's side of the family or some shit.

Janelle's body was what really got my attention. She was thick as hell, had a flat stomach even though she didn't work out every day, thick ass thighs, and a nice-sized butt.

Her breasts weren't the biggest, but they were a nice enough size. Then on top of that, her pussy was better than Tammy's. Yeah, that's fucked up, but it is what it is.

One day, when I had come over to see my son, she had just gotten out of the shower. She had on some lace underwear and a bra to match. I think she knew exactly what she was doing when she opened the door looking like a Victoria's Secret model. I couldn't keep my eyes off of her even though I was trying my hardest to. I knew Alani was at the crib waiting for me to get back, so I just wanted to see my son and dip, but Janelle had other plans though.

After I put Jr. to sleep, I was getting ready to leave. I was high as hell because I had popped two pills before I came over. I was already horny from staring at her in her underwear, and she knew that shit too. When I walked by her to leave, she stopped me and put her hand on my semi-erect penis. Without saying anything, she dropped to her knees and swallowed my whole entire dick. I was too shocked to stop her, plus the way her tonsils were feeling had me captivated. I hadn't had any pussy since Alani came home because I really just couldn't bring myself to do it. Knowing that she had gotten raped every day by that fuck nigga had me all in my feelings, so I just wouldn't touch her. I know, I was probably making her feel worse about the situation, but I just couldn't do it.

After Janelle swallowed all of my kids, I fucked her all over the house, and she was nasty as hell. She let me fuck her in every single hole, and she even let me cum on her face. She didn't have a problem with it at all, so I made sure I fucked her every time I came to see my son. I knew it was fucked up to be fucking my dead baby mother's mom, but right now, I didn't care about a lot of shit.

I knew Alani was thinking I was cheating on her. I hated to do this to her because I really did love that girl, but Janelle didn't mean shit to me. She was nothing more than a good nut. Alani was the one I wanted to marry and give me kids. That would all happen one day, after I was finished with Janelle.

Pulling up to Janelle's crib, I parked in her driveway and got out of the car. I had a key to her house because she gave me one. She told me that I should be able to come and go as I pleased since I was coming to see my son, and I didn't have a problem with it at all.

I walked into the house and Janelle was sitting on the couch watching TV. She looked happy as hell to see me, and she got up and came to give me a hug.

"I didn't expect for you to be back so soon." she said giving me a quick kiss on the lips.

"Jr. sleep?" I asked.

"Yes. I just put him down for a nap. You know what that means." she said licking her juicy lips. I knew exactly what she wanted. It was like she couldn't be in my presence without wanting the dick.

"Cook first. A nigga is hungry as hell." I said walking over to the couch then sitting down. I was expecting Alani to have breakfast made when I came home earlier, but she didn't. I was shocked, because she always cooked breakfast for me. No matter how mad she was at me. I still couldn't believe that I had put my hands on her, but I would find a way to make it up to her when I got home later.

About ten minutes later, Janelle came into the living room and handed me a plate full of bacon, eggs, and pancakes. Janelle's cooking skills weren't as good as Alani's, but it was better than nothing. I was just happy to be eating because my stomach was touching my back.

As soon as I was finished eating, Janelle was on her knees in front of me taking all of me inside her mouth. Her sex drive was high as hell, but I wasn't complaining. She made sure I never left her house horny, and that was why I fucked with her.

After I fucked Janelle in almost every position there was known to man, I put my clothes back on so that I could leave. I walked into my son's room, and he was still sleeping, so I kissed him on his forehead then made my way to the front door.

"Why are you in such a hurry to leave? Is your other bitch calling you or something?" Janelle asked with an obvious attitude. I didn't know why she had an attitude. She knew all about Alani. I made sure to tell her so she would know her place.

"Don't call her no bitch, aight? You knew what it was when we started fucking around so don't try to get your feelings involved now." I said leaving her standing there as I walked out of the house. I always felt bad after I left Janelle's house but not bad enough to stop fucking her. As long as Janelle and Alani never crossed paths, I think everything would be good.

When I got back to my place, it was quiet as hell. I just knew Alani would be in the kitchen drinking because she had been doing that a lot lately. I made my way upstairs so that I could take a shower, because I needed to wash Janelle off of me. I could've just taken a shower at her house, but I needed to leave. What happened between Alani and me earlier was really bothering me, and I needed to make things right. I didn't put my hands on women. I just wasn't that type of nigga. These pills had me trippin' earlier.

Alani wasn't in the room either. She was probably somewhere with Lena. I picked up the phone to call her but it went straight to voicemail. Alani never sent me to voicemail. Usually, she answered on the first ring. Maybe her phone was dead or some shit. I would try again after my shower.

I took a shower, then found something comfortable to put on. I sat down on the bed and called Alani again. I got the same result which was her voicemail. I called back three more times before I just gave up. I felt myself getting upset so I tried to calm myself down. I decided that I was just going to go to sleep and wait for her to bring her ass home. She better have a good ass reason to why her phone was going straight to voicemail.

As I got comfortable on the bed, something on the dresser caught my eye. It was a piece of paper, and next to it was Alani's engagement ring. *What the fuck?* I picked up the paper and couldn't believe what I was reading.

Carlos,

I can't do this with you anymore. I don't know what's going on with you, but you are not the man I fell in love with anymore. You letting the sun beat you home and coming in with hickeys on your neck was one thing. But putting your hands on me is just not okay. I can't be with a man who thinks it's okay to put his hands on me and cheat on me. I love myself too much and that's just not going to work. I'm sorry that I wasn't good enough for you. I'll always love you and maybe one day things can go back to how they used to be. Until then, I think it's best we go our separate ways.

Alani

I didn't know how to feel right now. I knew what I was doing was stupid, but I didn't think that Alani would actually leave me. She was my rib. Lately, I haven't been treating her right, and now she's gone, and I couldn't even be mad at anyone but myself. Ali had even warned me about what I was doing, but I didn't want to listen.

I balled the letter up and threw it at the wall. Then, I tried to call Alani one last time only to still get her voicemail. I was so mad right now, and I needed something to calm myself down, so I popped two more pills. I just couldn't believe that Alani was actually gone. This shit didn't even feel right.

I woke up from sleep that I never meant to have. My phone was on the dresser ringing so I picked it up to looked at the screen. For some reason, I was hoping that it was Alani, but it was Ali.

"Hello?" I said sleepily into the phone.

"Nigga, you sleep? Wake yo' ass up. We got business to tend to." he said.

"What kind of business you talking about?"

"That nigga Juice is down here for his birthday and wants us to hit the strip club with him." I looked at the clock, and it was now going on ten-thirty p.m. I really didn't feel like going anywhere, either. All I wanted to do was stay in the house and drink all my problems away. But, getting out of the house was probably the best thing for me to right now. I didn't need to be alone, because I would only keep thinking about Alani.

"Aight. I'll meet you there." I said then ended the call. As soon as I hung up with Ali, I checked my phone to see if I had any text messages or anything from Alani and of course I didn't. She really wasn't fucking with me, and it was all because of me. I had a couple of messages from Janelle and this bitch named Tamisha that I met in the mall one day, but all they wanted was some dick.

I threw the covers off of me and sat up in bed. I pulled two pills from out of the little plastic bag I had sitting on the dresser and just held them in my hand. They were the reason I was acting like this. They were the reason Alani didn't want to be with me anymore. I was addicted, and I needed to shake this habit ASAP. *Maybe I should start now. I should go flush all of these pills down the toilet. That's exactly what I should do.* But instead, I took the pills, popped them in my mouth, and got off of the bed. I'll stop taking the pills after I finish off this bag. *I'll be good after that.*

The club was packed for Juice's birthday, but that was expected though. He ran Jacksonville, and the part of Miami that I didn't. He was well-respected everywhere he went. There were so many bitches trying to get into our section just so they could be around that nigga. I shook my head at how thirsty these hoes were acting.

I looked over at Juice and he had two bitches giving him a lap dance. He was making it rain on them, and I knew they were happy as hell. Ali had some bitch sitting on his lap, and he was rubbing all over her thighs and shit. I swear this nigga just had a thing for strippers or some shit. He looked like he was ready to fuck her ass right here on the couch.

I was just chillin'. I thought being out of the house would keep my mind off of Alani, but I've been thinking about her non-stop since I got here. I pulled out another pill that I had in my pocket, then popped it in my mouth. I then took two shots of Henny and got up off of the couch. Just sitting here wasn't working for me. I needed to find me a fine ass bitch that I could take home with me tonight.

I didn't even get to make it out of our section before I was approached by a stripper, and she looked good as hell. She had a long rose pink weave that stopped at her ass, her body looked like she would've paid for it, but you could tell she was all natural, and she smelled good as hell.

"I saw you sitting over here looking lonely so I decided to come and keep you company." she smiled. I nodded my head and went to sit back down on the couch. I wasn't shocked that she had made herself comfortable on my lap.

"What's your name?" she asked.

"Los. What's yours?"

"When I'm here, my name is Roxy. But when I'm not here, you can call me Leslie." She kept smiling at me like she had just hit the jackpot or some shit.

"You leaving with me tonight right?" Her smiled faded, and she looked as if she was in deep thought.

"I don't know. I have a boyfriend." she had the nerve to say.

"I can't tell by the way you just made yourself comfortable on my lap like this." I said rubbing my hands all over her fat ass.

"Well, I couldn't resist. Your lap looked like it could use some company." she giggled.

"Tonight, I could use some company." She bit down on her bottom lip not knowing exactly if she wanted to come home with me or not. I honestly didn't give a fuck about her having a nigga. From the way she was pushing up on me, she obviously wasn't thinking about him.

"Okay, I'll go with you." she finally said.

"Cool." I said tapping her ass so that she could get off of my lap. I was ready to go, and all I was thinking about was what her mouth was capable of.

She seemed excited as hell about leaving with me. She was still smiling hard as hell and that shit was starting to get weird as hell.

"Are you going to let me ride in your car with you?" she asked. I looked at her like she was stupid. What kind of question is that?

"I wasn't gonna make you walk." I replied getting into the driver's side of my car. She smiled again and got in the passenger's seat.

"This car is so nice. I can't wait to see what your house looks like." Now she was really trippin' if she thought she was about to come to the crib. She had the game all fucked up. I chuckled and headed towards the nearest hotel. I wasn't trying to spend a lot of money on this broad because after tonight, she would be a thing of the past.

Pulling into the Quality Inn's parking lot, I could see Leslie's smile fade out of the corner of my eye. I laughed to myself because she really thought she was going to see where I laid my head at.

"I thought we were going to your place." she said once I found a park and cut the car off.

"Nah sweetheart, I don't even know you like that." She looked as if she wanted to say something, but then decided against it. I got out of the car and she followed me. She didn't bother putting on regular clothes when we left the club because I guess she thought she was about to come to my crib and people wouldn't see her. She still had on a black G-string, with a matching bra and some tall ass heels.

As we walked through the lobby, people were staring at the both of us, but I didn't give a fuck. I was too damn high to give a fuck about anything right now. I could tell that she was very uncomfortable with how people were staring at her, but I didn't know why though. She was a stripper; she did this shit for a living. She should be used to people looking at her body while she was half-naked.

"I wish you would've told me that we were coming to a hotel and not your house. I didn't even bring a change of clothes. I left my bag in my locker." she said once we got into the room. I really didn't give a fuck about nothing she was talking about.

"You should've known better. Why would I bring some random to the place I rest my head at?" I asked firing up a blunt.

"Random? Why are you treating me like I'm a hoe or some shit?" she said standing in front of me and folding her arms across her chest. I chuckled to myself because that's exactly what she was to me. I didn't say anything to her. I just pulled my dick out and looked up at her.

"It's not gonna suck itself." I said. She looked at me like she had an attitude, but she still dropped down to her knees and gently grabbed me in her hand. She carefully licked the tip before she put the whole thing in her mouth. She made eye contact with me the whole time and I had to bite down on my lip to keep from moaning. She was really good at what she was doing. She had me about to bust already, and it hadn't even been a full five minutes yet.

I grabbed the back of her head and forced her down further. When I felt the back of her throat, I thought I was gonna lose it. She didn't even gag or choke. I wasn't even expecting for it to be this good.

"Shit." I grunted feeling my nut rising. She started playing with my balls, and I couldn't take it anymore. I exploded all in her mouth, but she wasn't feeling that shit. She instantly spit everything out onto the floor, and I just shook my head at her childish ass.

"Why would you do that? You didn't even warn me or anything." she complained. I was starting to like her better when my dick was down her throat. I stood up and pulled a condom out of my pocket. Then, I came out of my pants, and she got on the bed and took off her G-string. I slid the condom on and spread her legs as far as they would go then entered her. As soon as I slid up in her, I was disappointed. She was dry as hell. She was moaning, making faces and doing all of that extra shit, and I wasn't enjoying this at all. I pulled out and flipped her over. Maybe it was the position we were in. I started fucking her from the back, but the shit was still the same.

"Ohhh, yesss! Right there!" she yelled. I had to think about the head she had just given me just to keep me hard, but it wasn't working. My dick went limp and I just gave up. I pulled out of her and went to go flush the dry ass condom down the toilet.

When I got back into the room, she was sitting in bed and had a confused look on her face.

"What's wrong?" she asked.

"Nothing, I got somewhere to be though, so I'll get up with you a little later." I told her putting my pants back on and heading towards the door.

"Really? So you're really just about to fuck me and not even stay the night? You really think I'm some type of hoe, huh?" she asked.

"You are." I said then left out of the room. I didn't know how she was going to get home, nor did I care. She was too damn young to have a dry ass pussy like that. She should really be ashamed of herself.

I got to my car and checked my phone to see if I had any missed calls from Alani. I didn't, but I was still hoping that she would start to miss me by now and maybe just want to talk. I guess not though. I shook my head at what I had just done with Leslie. This right here is why I'm single now. Instead of fucking bitches, I should be trying to get my life together. I needed Alani back ASAP. I feel like I can't function without her.

Chapter Sixteen

Draya

I sat on the bed in Ali's house waiting patiently for him to come home. He had been gone all day, and he wasn't answering his phone. I wanted to know where the hell he was and who he was with. I know one thing, he better not be with another bitch. I would be ready to kill him and her.

See, I knew exactly who Ali was when he came into the liquor store. My cousin Lena had told me all about his fine ass. She talked so much about him and his big ass dick, I started to want him for myself. He sounded like he was that nigga, and he definitely was. I was so happy I let him take my virginity, and I felt that that was the best decision I had ever made.

Growing up, Lena always got everything. She had a mom that actually loved her, she would get whatever she asked for, and even all the boys wanted her. Lena's body started developing at a young age and all the boys loved it. Boys wouldn't even pay any attention to me because I had no shape whatsoever. Lena had even won prom queen when we were still in high school. She knew I wanted to be prom queen more than anything in the world, but she ran for it anyway.

Lena was always winning growing up, but now the shoe was on the other foot, and it was I who was winning. I took her man from her and she didn't know how to act. I bet she's somewhere crying her eyes out about the whole situation. I smiled to myself just thinking about how hurt she probably is right now.

"What the fuck are you doing in my house? How the fuck did you even get in here?" Ali said snapping me out of my thoughts about Lena. Ali did not look pleased to see me at all. Well, he did kick me out the other day, but I had given him some time to cool down so he should be happy to see me right now.

"What do you mean, baby? You gave me a key." I said smiling at him. He didn't give me a key. I took his and had over fifty copies made just for back up. I put his back on his keychain, and he didn't even know a thing.

"I ain't never gave your delusional ass a key to my crib. Now, what the fuck are you doing here?" I could hear the annoyance in his voice, and I didn't understand why he was feeling some type of way towards me.

"I missed you. You didn't miss me? Why are you acting like this towards me?" I asked.

"Hell no I didn't miss you! Because of you, I might not ever get Lena back." Of course that's all he was thinking about. Why was she so damn special to these niggas? What did she have that I didn't? I didn't understand this at all.

"You don't need Lena. You have me. Don't I mean something to you?" He looked at me like he wanted to choke my ass, but then he just walked into the bathroom and shut the door behind him. He wasn't about to ignore me like I was nothing. I got up and went into the bathroom behind him. He was taking his clothes off and about to get in the shower, and he looked so damn good naked.

"Draya, take your ass home." he said. I dropped down to my knees and tried my hardest to deep throat him. I still wasn't very experienced because Ali was the only man I was fucking and had fucked. I was choking and my eyes were tearing up, but I didn't stop. I wasn't going to stop until Ali wanted me again.

"Damn Dray, just like that." he moaned. Something that I loved hearing. He grabbed the back of my head and started fucking my mouth. I hated when he did that, but I wasn't going to let him know that. I didn't want him to think that I was some boring bitch, so I closed my eyes and let him do his thing.

"I'm about to bust." he grunted before spilling all of his warm semen down my throat. I hated the taste of it, but I swallowed every time. Like I said, I wasn't about to be a boring ass bitch.

"Can I take a shower with you, daddy?" I asked standing to my feet. He smirked at me, and I took that as a yes. I quickly came out of my clothes and stepped in the shower, then he got in right behind me. We were in the shower fucking each other silly until the water got cold. I didn't mind the cold water at all, but he claimed it was making his dick soft, so we got out.

All he needed was some pussy because now he's treating me like he missed me. He was rubbing all over my booty making me feel like my butt was almost the same size as Lena's. He even gave me a foot massage, and I didn't even have to ask for it. I was really falling for this man. I just needed a way to get his mind off of Lena so he could fully focus on me and our relationship.

"Babe, could you take me to the mall? I could really use some new clothes." I said. I really did want a whole new wardrobe. I had been basically stalking Lena on social media and I wanted to start dressing just like her. I figured, the more I act like her then the more Ali will want me. It's the perfect plan.

"Right now?" he asked. I could tell he really didn't want to go anywhere, but at the same time, I didn't care. He had money that needed to be spent on me.

"Yes right now."

"You don't even need any new clothes. What's wrong with the ones that you already have?" I rolled my eyes because we could be in the car by now and on our way to the mall.

"Pleaseee?" I begged. He blew out a frustrated breath and gave in like I knew he would.

"We not about to be in this damn mall all day. I got shit to do later, aight?" he let me know as we got into his car. I smiled at him and nodded his head. We would be in the mall as long as I wanted to, but I didn't tell him that. I just sat back in my seat and enjoyed the ride to the mall with my man.

The first store I went to was Saks. They always had cute dresses online, but I had never really been in the store, because I didn't make enough money working at the liquor store to buy anything from there. Ali sat down on the bench and started playing on his phone. I didn't know why, but I had a feeling that he was texting other females. I wanted to slap the phone right out of his hand, but I didn't want to cause a scene in the mall.

I picked up an olive green strapless dress and smiled at it. Lena had this same exact dress because she posted a picture in it a while back. This color would look so good on me. My body wasn't as good as hers, but it was good enough. I held the dress up to my body, and I couldn't wait to wear it. Ali wouldn't be able to keep his hands off of me when I had this on.

"I don't even know why I always come in here. I swear, I have enough clothes already." I heard a familiar voice say. I looked up, and it was Lena walking with some fine ass light-skinned dude. What the fuck? Where does she be finding these niggas at? I looked over at Ali, and he was grilling Lena and whoever her new boo was. I wanted to slap him. Why was he worrying about her when he was there with me?

"Babe, do you think I would look good in this dress?" I said loud enough for Lena to hear. I wanted her to see me with Ali. I wanted her to know that he's still with me even after he found out that she and I were cousins.

"Yeah, it's straight." Ali said with his eyes still trained on Lena. I rolled my eyes because he didn't even look at the dress that I had in my hand.

"Oh hey, Draya. I got that same dress. I would give it to you but your ass isn't fat enough to fit in it and your imaginary boobs would have the dress falling down every two seconds." Lena said walking towards me. That's when I realized that I hated her. I hated everything about her. I wish she would have never been born.

"I see you move on fast." I said looking at her new nigga. Shit, I wanted him to myself too. Why couldn't I ever find these fine ass niggas with money before Lena did? What kind of curse did I have on me?

"And I see you're still busy with my leftovers." she laughed. "You'll never be me, baby. Stop trying." she said. I didn't have anything to say because I really did want to be her. I wanted her whole entire life. I wish she could see how it feels to be second all of the time.

"Hey Ali." she said smiling at him. She was just being petty now. She knew damn well she didn't want to talk to him.

"This is how we doing it now?" Ali said standing to his feet. He was talking to whoever this mystery man was.

"Fuck you talking 'bout, bruh?" the mystery man said.

"You know damn well what I'm talking about. Everybody in Miami knows Lena is my girl. Nigga, you seen us together at Alani's birthday party!" Ali yelled.

158

"And? She's obviously where she wants to be my nigga. She ain't your girl no more either. Your girl is right there, and if I've been hearing right, that's also Lena's cousin. You foul as fuck for that shit." Ali didn't have anything to else to say. He looked over at me and looked like he was disgusted. He then turned and walked right out of the store without telling me to come on or anything.

"Good luck. You're going to need it. Oh, and ask him how his baby mama is doing and if she's had the baby yet." Lena said laughing. She grabbed her nigga's hand, and they walked out of the store too. This was news to me. Who the fuck was his baby mama? He never said anything to me about him having a child on the way or anything. I wanted to cry because I was so mad. I held back my tears and walked out of the store to go find Ali. This nigga was so full of shit. I don't know why niggas think they can just play with your feelings like this.

I spotted Ali sitting on another bench looking like he had just lost his best friend. That shit pissed me off. Why was he so stuck on Lena? Why did he think so highly of her? Why couldn't he just get over her and move on with me? I was so much better than her! Why couldn't nobody see that?

"Why did you just leave like that?" I asked him.

"Because I wasn't trying to end up in jail for killing that nigga." he said.

"Who's your baby mama? Nigga, you got a baby on the way and you didn't even tell me?" I asked feeling the tears coming back. Ali looked at me then started laughing. That wasn't the reaction that I was expecting at all. What the hell did he think was so funny?

"Why would I tell you that? You're not my bitch. You're not my girl. We just fuck. Stop trying to make us something we're not." he said standing up. He had really just said that I'm not his girl. Then why would he act like it? This is what I didn't understand about him.

"So, I don't mean anything to you?" I asked with my voice trembling.

"You do when my dick is down your throat. But other than that, nope. Now let's go. I'm tired of being here." he said making my heart shatter into a million pieces. I couldn't stop the tears from falling. I thought Ali had feelings for me, but I guess I was wrong. I started walking behind him until we reached his car. He didn't say anything else to me, and it only made me cry harder.

"Aye, can you shut up with that crying shit? I need to make a phone call." Hehe said. I couldn't believe how nasty he was being towards me right now. I hadn't done anything to him at all. Yeah, I knew about him and Lena, but who cares? Why can't he let the shit go? Lena has moved on, so why can't he do the same?

"What's good, Trina? I ain't heard from you in a little minute." he said into the phone. He was really talking to another bitch while I was in the car with him.

"I can call my baby mama to check up on her. Shit, I didn't think that would be a problem. You had the baby yet?" So this was the baby mama Lena was talking about.

"You had the baby two days ago and didn't think to call me? So fuck me right? I don't get to see the birth of my child because you wanna be all in your feelings and shit? What hospital you at? I'm about to be up there, aight?" he said then ended the call. I looked at him, and he acted like he couldn't feel me staring.

"I'm not about to go with you to see another bitch, Ali!" I yelled. He really had me fucked up right now. Who the hell did he think he was?

"I know you're not. I'm dropping your ass off at home." he said. I was starting to think that he really got a kick out of hurting my feelings or something. He kept doing it like it was nothing. I just shook my head and looked out of the window for the rest of the ride.

I didn't expect for him to bring me back to my apartment. I thought he was going to drop me off at his place then I was going to wait for him to get back. I didn't want to be at my apartment; I was going to be lonely as hell here.

"Why didn't you take me back to your place?" I asked.

"Why would I do that when you got your own place to go to?" he said looking down at his phone.

"What the fuck is your problem today? Why are you acting like such an asshole?" I asked feeling the tears stinging my eyes again. I didn't want to cry in front of him because it made me feel like I was weak and I hated that. I just wished he would stop treating me like this. It's all Lena's fault. He was perfectly fine with me until we ran into Lena.

"Why are you still in my car?" he asked looking at me this time. I didn't have anything else to say to him after that. Everything that came out of his mouth hurt me, and I couldn't take it anymore. I got out his car and made sure I slammed his door shut. He smiled at me, then drove off. He didn't even wait to see if I made it into my apartment safely or not. I mean, yeah it was still daytime, and I lived in a nice community, but it was the principle.

I slowly walked up to my apartment and unlocked the door. Now that I was alone, I could cry as much as I wanted to. I went to go lie down on my bed and I sobbed lightly. All I wanted was for Ali to love me like I loved him, and he was acting like it was such a hard thing for him to do. I knew he had feelings for me. There was no way that I didn't mean shit to him. He had to be lying when he said that. I prayed that he was lying when he said that.

I decided that I was just going to give him his space for a couple of days before I went back over to his house to see him. I was going to show him that I was so much better than Lena. I was going to help him get over her, so I wouldn't be giving up on Ali anytime soon. I was going to be his woman, and he was going to be my man. It might take some time, but it was going to happen if it was the last thing I did.

Chapter Seventeen

Ali

A nigga was mad as hell seeing Lena in the mall with that Jaxon nigga. She looked like she was happy as hell holding his hand and shit. I couldn't believe that's who she was fucking with now. The thought of him touching her at all had me ready to body his ass. I wanted to do it right there in the mall, but I wasn't trying to go to jail. I was enjoying my freedom.

When he brought up Draya being Lena's cousin, I wanted to strangle Draya. This is all her fault. I should've never invited her to my room that day I saw her at the liquor store. She was trying to act like she was so innocent, but the whole time she knew exactly what she was doing. I told myself that I was going to leave her alone so that I could focus on getting Lena back. Her good ass pussy and head had my head gone. I forgot all about Lena and now Lena probably really thinks Draya and I are serious.

I shook my head as I made my way to the hospital. I couldn't believe this bitch Trina had the baby and didn't even call a nigga. Yeah, I didn't think the baby was mine, but even if it was, I would've liked to be able to see the baby come into this world. That right there let me know that I wasn't the father of her child, but I was going to get a DNA test done anyway.

When I got to the hospital, I told the lady at the desk who I was there to see, and she told me what floor and room number Trina was in. I was ready to get this over with. If this baby wasn't mine, I was going to be done with Trina for good. I should've been done with her a long time ago, but I was too busy being stupid.

Trina was sitting up in bed holding the baby in her arms. I didn't know if she had a boy or a girl, because all I cared about was getting this DNA test done. She looked at me and rolled her eyes like I had done something wrong to her ass. I ignored her and held my arms out so that I could hold the baby. She was hesitant at first, but she handed the baby to me. From the pink blanket, I knew it was a girl.

"What's her name?" I asked.

"Stephanie." she said. Looking down at this baby, I knew she wasn't mine. This was a white man's child. She had blond hair and blue eyes. I just shook my head at Trina and gave her child back to her. She thought she was going to trap me, but it didn't work.

"Does the real father of your child know he's the father?" I asked. She shook her head no, then started crying.

"I'm so sorry, Ali. I know I shouldn't have popped up at your house like that. I just heard how much you talked about your new girlfriend, and it made me jealous. You never talked about me like that to anyone. You would bring her up right after we had sex. Who wants to hear that? I didn't want to hear the man I loved talking about his new bitch." she said.

"Don't call her a bitch. Her name is Lena." I corrected her.

"I know what the fuck her name is. You used to call me her while we were fucking. Do you know how that made me feel, Ali? At one point, I thought about killing myself. But then I found out that I was pregnant. To be honest, I was fucking the both of you at the same time so I didn't know who the father was. I was just hoping it was you. I wanted it to be you to be you so bad. Then you would be in my life forever."

"No, I would've been in my child's life forever. Not yours. What we had is over and done with. Especially after you had that nigga up in the shit I was paying for. How did he feel about not being the father?" I asked remembering that nigga who was in her crib that one time I went over to see her.

"Not too good. He left me and told me to lose his number. I've lost everyone that I loved. I don't want to go back to that nasty ass house that my mom lives in. Half the time, she's too damn high to even realize that I'm in the house with her. There're roaches and rats everywhere. I don't want my daughter growing up around that. I don't know what I should do." she said shaking her head.

"Well for one, you could get a job." I said. Trina was lazy as hell. She didn't want to work at all. She was always

165

looking for a come up off of a nigga. She had it with me, but she fucked all of that up.

"I guess I have to now. I don't have any money and now I have a daughter. I fucked up everything." I wasn't trying to hear her sad ass story anymore. This shit was depressing as hell, and she had no one to blame but herself.

"It'll all work out for you. I'll see you around." I said kissing her on her forehead then leaving out of the room. Now I know why she didn't call me after she had that damn baby. She knew for a fact that it wasn't mine, and she was probably embarrassed as hell. I was happy that the baby wasn't mine though, because the only person I wanted to have my kids was Lena. I was going to make sure she was the one to give me my first born too. I wasn't having babies with none of these bitches I was fucking. Especially Draya. I needed to get rid of her ass anyway.

Draya was a cool chick, but I felt like she was crazy. Like today, when I came home and she was just sitting there on my bed. I never gave her a key to my crib. The only person who actually had a key was Lena, and I'm pretty sure she doesn't even have it anymore. I didn't want to be mean to Draya, but I feel like that was the only way I could get through to her. I'm not trying to be in a relationship with her at all. If anything, all I want to do is fuck and go on about my day.

I got in my car and headed towards Los' crib. I wonder if he knew that Lena was fucking with Jaxon now. Maybe

Alani told him or some shit. Either way, I was pissed about it. I know I fucked up, but I didn't expect for Lena to get with his ass. I guess I just wanted her to wait for me until I got my shit together. I don't know what the fuck I was thinking when I was fucking other bitches while we were together. There aren't really a lot of things that I regret in life, but choosing those bitches over Lena was something I had been regretting since it happened.

Pulling up to Los' crib, I saw Juice's car in the round driveway too. *I wonder what this nigga is doing over here.* I got out of my car and quickly jogged into the house. The smell of weed smacked me in the face as soon as I got through the front door. These niggas were sitting on the couch smoking and drinking and had bitches on their laps. What the fuck did Los have going on? Alani would probably kill this nigga if she came home and seen what he was doing.

"What's good, y'all?" I asked sitting on the opposite couch.

"What's good, nigga? I didn't even hear you come in the house." Juice said. His eyes were so damn low, I didn't even know how he could see me. I looked at Los who was rubbing all over the chick that was on his lap like he was single and shook my head. This nigga didn't care about shit.

"Los, what you got going on, man?" I asked. He looked at me and shrugged his shoulders.

"What you talking about?"

"Why you got this bitch on your lap like you're not in a full relationship?"

"Fuck that bitch." he scoffed. I didn't expect for him to say that. He didn't play about anyone calling Alani a bitch and here he was doing it. I didn't know what to say.

"What makes you say that? That's fucked up, Los."

"She left, so I'm free to do whatever I want." That was news to me. Alani was head over heels for Los' stupid ass. I wonder why she left him.

"She left? Why?"

"Because I like fucking other bitches and she didn't like that shit, so she left. Shit, she can be replaced." he said shrugging his shoulders. I wish he could hear how stupid he sounded right now.

"Los, you trippin', my nigga. That was your fiancé. How you gonna sit here and act like you don't love her? You acting like this bitch on your lap is more important than your relationship." I said feeling myself getting upset.

"Your fiancé? You didn't tell me you were engaged to that bitch." the girl on Los' lap said with an attitude.

"I don't have a fiancé. I'm single and I can do what I want." he said to her. I couldn't believe this nigga. Two months ago, he could barely function because he thought Alani was dead, but now he was acting like she never meant shit to him. I didn't understand. I just shook my head because soon enough he would realize how much he really needed Alani in his life.

"Well, anyway nigga, Lena is fucking with Jaxon now." I said to him. He looked at me and started laughing.

"Damn. I didn't expect for her ass to move on so quickly." he said. I didn't either. I didn't expect for any of this shit to happen.

"Oh, and that Draya bitch I've been fucking with is her cousin. Shit is all fucked up right now man. How the hell am I gonna get Lena back now that she knows I was fucking her cousin." This whole situation was fucked up.

"Shit, she'll be aight. Fuck these bitches." I didn't even know why I even bothered bringing my ass over here. Los always used to be the one I came to for advice, but right now, he was really trippin'. I wasn't feeling this shit at all. I watched as Los gently removed the girl from his lap, then reached for the small bag of pills that was on the table. He took two out of the bag and put them in his mouth.

That's what was wrong with this nigga. He was addicted to popping pills. I didn't even know what kind of pills they were, but he was a totally different nigga when he took them. I couldn't believe it. I thought he would've stopped popping them shits by now.

"You just popped two of those like thirty minutes ago. Don't you think you've had enough?" the girl said to him.

"Mind yo' fucking business. I'm a grown ass man. I can handle myself." he snapped. *Should I say something? Or should I let him continue so he can see for himself that he's on a pathway to destruction?*

"Los, let me holla at you real quick." I said standing up. He looked at me for a minute like he didn't want to get up, but he eventually got up and followed me into the kitchen.

"What's going on with you?" I asked.

"Shit. Living life, getting money, fucking bitches. Life is good right now." he said.

"No nigga, I'm talking about you popping pills and shit. You supposed to be selling them shits, not taking them. They're fucking you up." I said. He just laughed though.

"I'm good. I just like the way the pills make me feel. I've been taking them for a while now and I'm good."

"You're not good. You were cheating on your girl, you start fucking your baby mama's mom, and you don't give a fuck about anything anymore. You need to stop taking those pills."

"I'm good. I can quit when I want." he said going in the refrigerator and grabbing a beer. He kept telling me that he was good, but it was obvious he wasn't. I needed for him to see that what he was doing was slowly killing him.

"When's the last time you talked to your mom?" he shrugged his shoulders. That right there is how I know these pills were fucking him up. He loved his mom. He wouldn't go longer than a week without talking to her.

"That's fucked up, Carlos. These pills mean more to you than your own family?" I asked him. He looked at me with those glossy ass eyes and then chuckled.

"They don't give a fuck about me. Nobody gives a fuck about me except for these bitches that I'm fucking. My own girl didn't even care enough to stay with my ass. She didn't give a fuck that I was addicted to pills. She was just mad because I was fucking other bitches. So fucking what! It's not that serious." I didn't even say anything back to him. This nigga was really trippin' if he thought his mom and Alani didn't care about him. It was obvious that this nigga didn't want any help. Especially my help.

"Aight. I'll holla at you later." I told Los. I turned to walk out of the house, and he went right back to his bitch that was sitting on the couch. He was going to see soon that this is not what he wants out of life. I can't make him want to do the right thing. I just hoped he realized it before it was too late.

Chapter Eighteen

Lena

I had to admit, seeing Ali in the mall with Draya hurt like hell. He knew that she was my cousin, but he still chose to fuck with her. I had really been missing him a lot lately. I just didn't understand why I wasn't good enough for him. Why did he have to go out and fuck other bitches? But the real question is, why did he have to go out and fuck my cousin. Just thinking about them two together had me ready to kill the both of them, but I wasn't a killer.

"Lani, you have to get out of this bed. You can't spend the rest of your life here." I told Alani. She was living with Jaxon now ever since she left Los. She hadn't been herself at all. All she did was drink, cry, and sleep. It's been about two weeks since the break-up, and she was still taking it hard. I hated seeing her like this. I was used to her being happy all the time, and I couldn't stand this sad ass Alani. She got on my damn nerves.

"Go away." she said to me. She had the covers over her head and some sad ass music playing on Pandora. She wasn't doing anything but making herself feel worse than she already did. I walked into her room and turned off the music. There were empty Hennessy bottles all over the floor. I shook my head and pulled the covers from over her head. Her hair was a complete mess, her eyes were puffy as hell and red, she had bags underneath her eyes, and she looked like she hadn't slept in days.

"Get up, let's go shopping or something." I said.

"No. I'm fine laying here."

"No you're not. Please, just get up. I don't like seeing you like this. Let's go out and find you a new nigga to help you get over this one." I said then laughed at my own joke. That's exactly what I was doing with Jaxon. I knew I didn't really want a relationship with him, but he was wonderful in bed. I smiled just thinking about it.

"I don't want a new nigga. All they do is ruin your life." she said.

"No they don't." I said. She sat up and looked at me, and she looked terrible. I really wished I could just hug her and take all of the pain away.

"Get dressed. We're going to a party." I told her.

"Who's party? Where is it at? I don't want to be around a lot of people." I rolled my eyes at her complaining. She used to jump up at the mention of a party. Now, she's complaining about being around a lot of people.

"Girl, just get up. We need to do something to that head of yours. And you need to find something cute to wear." I said kissing her on her cheek. She rolled her eyes but threw the covers off of her and got out of the bed. I was happy as hell that she was finally getting out of the house, so I walked out of her room and into the room Jaxon and I had been sharing. He was getting dressed to go to his club. I loved the way he looked in a suit.

He looked at me and smirked. "It's not polite to stare." he said.

"I wouldn't be staring if you didn't look so good." He walked over to me and gave me a kiss on my lips.

"You trying to start some shit and I got somewhere to be."

"Yeah, you gotta go see your other bitches in the club." I said rolling my eyes. Jaxon and I weren't together or anything, but I still didn't like the thought of him entertaining other bitches.

"How many times do I have to tell you that you're the only bitch I got?" I pushed him then went to go sit on the bed.

"I am not a bitch." I said and folded my arms across my chest.

"I know, I was kidding. Stop being a big baby. I'll be back later, though. Don't have too much fun at that party shit without me." he said kissing me again then leaving the room. Shit, I was about to have so much fun without him. I planned on getting drunk as hell tonight, and I was going to do the same for Alani. She needed to get out of the house and have some fun for once.

After Jaxon left, I quickly jumped in the shower and brushed my teeth again. I knew exactly whose party it was that we were going to, but I didn't want to tell Alani because then she really wouldn't go with me. The party didn't start until ten, and it was only seven, so that meant we had plenty of time to get Alani's hair done and find her something to wear. It was a pool party, so I already knew that I was just going to wear some shorts and a swimsuit top, but I didn't know how Alani felt about that.

I threw on some leggings and a tank top then went into the room Alani was staying in. I was glad to see that she was already up and dressed. She was sitting on the bed rolling up.

"Girl, come on. There will be plenty of that at the party." I told her.

"Okay, but are we at the party right now?"

"Bitch, bring yo' ass. You really need your hair done. It looks terrible." She looked up at me and rolled her eyes, because she knew it was true. She hadn't done anything to her hair since the breakup and you could really tell.

She got up off of the bed, slid some flip-flops on, and followed me to my car. I could tell that she wasn't in the mood to do anything, but I didn't care. I was tired of this boring ass Alani. She needed to start being boring after she had kids, not right now while she's single and free to do whatever it is that she wants.

When we got to the hair salon, it didn't take long at all. All they did was wash it, blow dry it, and straighten it. She was looking better already, and I was glad, too.

"Where are you taking me now?" she asked once we got back into the car.

"The mall." I smiled at her. She rolled her eyes at me.

"I don't need a new outfit. I got plenty of clothes at Jaxon's house." This is how I knew she was trippin'. Alani loved to go shopping no matter how many clothes she had. A lot of her clothes still had the price tags on them and everything, but that didn't stop her from buying even more clothes that she knew she wasn't going to wear.

"Girl shut up. You need a new swimsuit, because I saw the one that you got and it's not what's up." I told her.

"What the hell do I need a swimsuit for?"

"Because it's a pool party silly. It's going to be fun, I promise." She rolled her eyes again.

"If the party isn't jumping in the first ten minutes, then I'm leaving. I don't care if I have to walk home." she said, and I knew she was serious as hell. I didn't say anything else to her, because I knew that she was going to enjoy the party because of who was throwing it.

Once we were in the mall, I went into a store that I knew had cute bathing suits. Alani was still acting like she wasn't excited about going, but I knew once a little bit of liquor got into her system, her attitude would change. I was so mad that Los had her feeling this way. I actually wanted them to work out, but now I was slowly starting to dislike him. He was causing my girl so much hurt and pain, and I wasn't here for it. She deserved someone who was all about her, not all about her and every other bitch that throws the pussy at him. I shook my head at my thoughts.

"I like this one. Now, can we go?" Alani said. She was holding a baby pink thong bikini.

"You sure you want this one?" I asked.

"Yes. I'm positive. Now, let's go." she said. I wasn't about to argue with her at all. She was going to get herself into some trouble with that tonight. We went to go pay for the swimsuit, then we were on our way back to Jaxon's house so that we could get ready.

When Alani walked into my room with her swimsuit on, I was shocked. I already knew that she was going to look good in it, but I wasn't expecting for her to look this good. She looked like a model for real. Her body was to die for. Her boobs looked like they were about to pop out of her little bikini top, but she didn't seem to care. She turned around and modeled for me.

"Is it too much? Do you think I look slutty?" she asked.

"Not at all. You look good as hell. You might take everyone's nigga tonight." I said and she laughed. I was so serious though.

"I don't want to take anyone's nigga. I'm trying to stay away from those." she said. I heard what she was saying, but I doubt that was going to happen. Everyone was going to be on her tonight, because she was looking that good.

By the time I had finished getting ready, it was time for us to go. Alani had put on some jean shorts like me because she said she felt naked. She's the one who wanted to get a swimsuit with the ass part out. That was her fault.

"I need something to drink." Alani said when we were pulling out of the driveway.

"There will be plenty to drink at the party." I told her. She chuckled and pulled a small bottle of Hennessy out of her purse. What the fuck?

"Bitch, you really keep a bottle in your purse?"

"Yes. You never know when you might need a drink, so I keep a bottle on me at all times.

"Girl, you done turned into an alcoholic." I remember at one point when Alani couldn't drink. She could barely drink wine. Now she was pulling bottles and shit out of her purse.

"I'm not an alcoholic. I only drink when I want to." she lied.

"No, you drink every damn day. You drink before you even eat breakfast. I think you should slow down on the drinking." I told her honestly. I did feel like she was drinking too much. Most of the time, she was in the house drinking and wasn't anywhere embarrassing herself, but for future references, what if she decided to go out to the club by herself and got sloppy drunk? What if she went home with a total stranger? What if she got raped by that stranger? I didn't want anything bad to happen to her.

"I'm fine. I can stop drinking whenever I feel like it." she said. That's what everyone says, but then they aren't able to quit. I let it go for now, but best believe I was going to bring it back up later. Hopefully, she could stop when she wanted to though.

We finally arrived at the party, and I was shocked as hell at how big the house was. It was damn near the same size as Los' estate. I looked over at Alani, and I could tell that she was thinking the same thing.

"Whose party did you say this was again?" she asked.

"Someone that I met while we were in Jacksonville. Now, come on. I'm ready to turn up." I said getting out of the car. I couldn't wait to see how tonight turned out. I was going to make sure Alani had fun. She really did deserve it.

Chapter Nineteen

Alani

I really didn't want to be at this party. I just wanted to lay underneath my covers and listen to sad ass music for the rest of the night. I was glad that Lena was trying to make me feel better by getting me out of the house, but I still felt like shit. It had been two weeks and Carlos hadn't even tried to contact me. I haven't gotten any calls, text messages, or anything, and I was starting to think that he was glad that I was gone.

I was on his Facebook page the other day, and I saw this bitch that kept tagging him in pictures. At first, it was just pictures of him and his son, so I didn't think anything of it, but then the pictures changed to the bitch sitting on his lap and kissing him on his cheek. I did my research and figured out that she is his baby mama's mother, but I knew they were fucking. Why the hell was she on his lap and kissing him like they were in a relationship or something? That's the most disgusting shit ever. How are you going to be fucking your dead daughter's baby daddy? Hoes these days.

I couldn't believe that's who he was spending his time with. He probably wanted to be a family and shit with them, so I was going to let him. I wasn't going to stay where I wasn't wanted. I just wished that it didn't hurt so bad. I loved that man with everything in me and he goes and does me like that? Niggas ain't shit.

Walking into this party, the music was blasting, and there were niggas and bitches everywhere. It looked like it was going to be fun, but the only thing I was worried about was getting drunk. I felt a lot better when I was drunk. Maybe after I found something to drink, I could enjoy myself more.

As I was walking into the kitchen, I was getting lustful stares from the niggas and hateful ones from the bitches. That was expected though, because I was looking good as hell. I ignored them all as I went into the kitchen where I saw all the liquor bottles, and I got excited as I approached them. I decided that I was just going to get a beer because I couldn't find any of the cups. What kind of shit was that? How are you gonna have all this liquor with no cups?

"Juice, where are all of the cups?" I heard a girl yell beside of me. I looked over at her, and she looked like she was fucked up. She was skinny as hell with long ass blond weave and she had on an all-white, one-piece swimsuit.

"Look in the cabinet." I heard a familiar voice say. I didn't mean to stare, but I just couldn't help it. That was the effect that he had on me. He had the nerve to not be wearing a shirt showing off all of his tattoos.

"Alani." he said smiling at me.

"Oh, hey Juice." I said trying to act like I wasn't interested. I felt like I had been set up. Lena knew whose party this was. That's why she wouldn't give a name when I asked.

"You look good as hell." he said looking at my chest. The little blond chick didn't look too pleased with how he was lusting over me.

"Come on, Juice. Let's go back outside." she said. It was obvious that she wanted Juice all to herself, but he was too stuck on me.

"You go ahead. I'll be out there in a minute." She rolled her eyes, but she left out of the kitchen.

"Are you enjoying the party?" he asked. I shrugged my shoulders.

"If I was drunk then I surely would be enjoying it." I stated honestly. He laughed then went to the cabinet to get the plastic cups out.

"Well, drink up then. I'll see you around." he said. I watched him as he walked out of the kitchen, and he was so fine. *I wonder if he's still in a relationship.*

"I saw you talking to Julian." Lena said when she came into the kitchen.

"Shut up, bitch. You set me up. You knew damn well it was his party." I said pouring me some Hennessy in a cup.

"I know, but I had to do something to get your mind off of Los." she said. I rolled my eyes at the mention of his name. He didn't even care about me, but it was okay. I could act the same way he was acting.

183

It didn't take long for me to get drunk. I was throwing back shots like they were water. Lena didn't drink that much because she was driving home tonight. I didn't care though. I didn't want to remember anything from this night. I had a sudden urge to pee, so I stumbled my way to the bathroom. It seemed like it took me forever to get there, then there was a long ass line. My bladder was about to explode, and I knew this wasn't the only bathroom that he had in this big ass mansion, so I made my way upstairs. Hopefully, I didn't get lost on my way back or something.

I found the bathroom as soon as I got upstairs and I basically ran to it. Happy was an understatement as I sat on the toilet and released my bladder. Once I was finished, I flushed the toilet, washed my hands, and left out of the bathroom. I didn't expect for Juice to be standing right there as soon as I got out of the bathroom.

"Are you following me?" I giggled.

"I had to make sure you were good. You ran up the stairs so I thought you were sick or some shit." he said. I wanted to reach out and touch his bare chest because it was right there and it was looking good as hell. Everything about him was looking good as hell, but I had to look away from him to stop all of the nasty thoughts that were running through my head.

"Oh, I just had to use the bathroom. There was a long line downstairs." He nodded his head letting me know that he understood why I came all the way upstairs. I hope he didn't think I was trying to rob him or some shit. I wasn't that type of female. Well, I wouldn't steal from him.

"This is a nice house. Do you use it for when you're here visiting?" I asked.

"Nah, I'm moving back. I was born and raised in Miami. I just moved to Jacksonville to make more money. I'm here to stay, though. I missed it too much." I couldn't help but smile when he told me that he had moved back from Jacksonville. That meant that I would be able to see him more often.

"Oh that's what's up." I let him know.

"Yeah, you should stay the night with me." he said out of nowhere. I looked at his face to see if he was joking, but he was dead serious, and I didn't know how I felt about that.

"I don't know. I came here with Lena and I have to make sure she gets home safely." He chuckled lightly.

"Stop making excuses. Lena is good. She'll get home safe, I promise."

"I don't have any clothes either." I quickly said.

"It's all good. You won't be needing them anyway." he said smirking. I looked away from him again and thoughts of Carlos and his new bitch invaded my mind. Bitch ass nigga.

"Okay, I'll spend the night." I told him, and he smiled big as hell.

"Good. I'm about to make everyone leave so we can spend time together." he said turning to walk back down the stairs. I walked right behind him wanting to go get me something else to drink.

"Juice, where have you been? I've been looking for you." that same skinny blond said walking up to us. Her whole attitude changed when she saw me standing beside him. She rolled her eyes and folded her arms.

"I know you're not fucking her like I'm not here!" she yelled. She was about to cause a scene for no reason.

"And if I am? That shit is none of your business. Don't think you're somebody because I let you suck my dick before the party started. I'm a grown ass man. I can do whatever the fuck I want to in my fucking house, Amanda." he said putting her in her place. *Oh, so Amanda is her name.* I thought to myself.

I could tell that Amanda was embarrassed by the look on her face. She looked at him then her eyes shifted to me. I couldn't help but laugh. She really thought she was somebody.

"So why would you even invite me to your party knowing you planned on sleeping with someone else tonight?" she asked sounding sad as hell. I just shook my head at her desperate ass. It's obvious that he doesn't want her. She's nothing more than a quick fuck to him, but she thinks they're going to be in a relationship or something.

"Because I can do that. Now get the fuck outta my face." I couldn't believe how he was just talking to her like she was nothing. I could never let a man talk to me like that. I had too much self-respect.

"I'm going to let my daddy know how you're treating me. Let's see what he has to say about this." she threatened him, but again, he just laughed in her face.

"I don't give a fuck about your daddy. What that nigga gon' do to me? Stop me from making money? Hell nah. That nigga needs me more than I need him, so tell his bitch ass. I'm still going to be fucking someone who isn't you." I could see the tears that were threatening to fall from her eyes. She didn't say anything else. She just turned to walk away. Really, that's what she should've done to begin with.

"That was fucked up." I told him. He shrugged his shoulders. This nigga didn't care about shit. For some reason, that was a turn on for me. I liked how he handled people. He held so much authority. I poured me another shot, and I was probably going to have a terrible hangover in the morning, but right now I didn't even care. I was glad that Lena made me leave the house today. I was really enjoying myself.

Once everyone left Juice's house, he led me upstairs to his massive room, and his bed was huge. I felt like a little kid right now because I really just wanted to jump on it until I got tired, but I decided against it. He would probably put me out of his house if I started doing that.

He handed me one of his large tee shirts to put on, then he went to get in the shower. I quickly changed from my bathing suit into his shirt and it smelled just like him. I made myself comfortable on his bed and turned the TV on. Before I knew it, I was out like a light.

I woke up the next morning with a banging headache. I sat up in bed and realized that I wasn't at Jax's house. I couldn't really remember anything that happened last night and that was really bothering me. I looked to my left to see Juice sleeping so peacefully. Like always, he looked good enough to eat.

I started to remember a little bit. I came to his party, got sloppy drunk, and then passed out. I couldn't remember if we had sex or not.

"Stop staring at me like that. That shit is weird as hell." he said without even opening his eyes.

"How did you know that I was staring at you?"

"I can feel it. I don't like when people stare at me while I'm sleep." he said opening his eyes to look at me. I didn't feel good at all. I didn't want to get out of the bed, but I knew he probably didn't want me to stay here all day.

"How you feeling? You got drunk as hell last night." he said getting out of the bed and walking into his bathroom to use it.

"I feel like shit. I need to stop drinking for real." I said shaking my head. "Did we have sex last night?" he walked back into his room and sat on the bed.

"I wanted to. I was thinking about that shit while I was in the shower, but when I got out, you were knocked out. I even picked your heavy ass up to put you on the right side of the bed and you didn't wake up at all."

"I am not heavy!" I said to him.

"Your ass was last night. Shit, I was drunk too, but unlike you, I can actually hold my liquor." he chuckled.

"I can hold mine too. I just drunk too much last night. Now, I'm regretting it." I said lying back down on the pillow. I was a little bummed out that me and him didn't have sex, but it was probably for the best. Since I was so drunk, I wouldn't have remembered it anyway.

"I'll be out of your hair soon. I just want this headache to ease up a little bit." I told him. He laid back down beside of me.

"It's all good. You can stay as long as you would like."

"You sure? I don't want to be in the way or anything. What if you want to have other females over?"

"Then I'll bring them over, but I don't need any other females if you're here." He looked at me and I looked away. If I didn't know any better, I would say that Juice was feeling me. He shouldn't though. My heart is still with someone else, so it wouldn't be fair to even think about pursuing anything with him. I didn't say anything back to him. I just closed my eyes. Hopefully, this headache would go away soon. When it did, I was going to take my ass back to Jaxon's house.

Chapter Twenty

Londyn

I was mad as hell that my plan didn't work like I wanted it to. I knew I should've just killed Alani instead of kidnapping her, and I was regretting everything that happened now. I just knew that I would be dead by now. I was sure Los wasn't going to stop until he had me killed. I didn't want to live while constantly looking over my shoulder, so I just left Miami altogether. I was now in Atlanta because I knew Los probably wouldn't think to find me there.

After I got away from Alani's little sidekick, I went back to Darius' house. I had to let him know that we needed to leave ASAP. I didn't think that I would go to his house and he would already be dead, though. There was blood everywhere and his brains were splattered all over the wall. I didn't care that much for Darius, but it was still a sad situation. Now his kids were going to grow up without their parents being that Jasmine was dead too.

I didn't know what to do. There was too much blood to try and clean up, and I never disposed of a dead body before. I made sure to grab everything that was valuable out of the house, then I burnt it down. I didn't even stay to watch. I didn't have time for that. By now, Alani had told Los everything and they were probably looking for me. I wasn't ready to die just yet, so I had to get out of Miami.

I decided that once I got to Atlanta, I was just going to start my life over. I needed a way to get money, and I needed it to be quick. I couldn't dance at all, so stripping was out of the question. I did the next best thing. I found me a nigga with money who didn't mind spending it all on me. Yeah, he had a wife but I didn't care about any of that. The only thing I was worried about was this nigga paying my bills. All I had to do was have sex with him and he would give me stacks of money.

His name was Anthony and he was a judge. I ran into him when I was trying to check into a hotel. He was coming off of the elevator while I was trying to get on it. He was in his late forties, but he didn't look like it. He was actually a really nice looking man. He invited me to the bar with him and we hit it off instantly, but I never thought I would want to be with a man that was twice my age.

"Babe, I need some money." I told Anthony once we were finished having sex. He had bought me a house and a new car. He really had money to blow and I loved it.

"I just gave you some money yesterday. What do you need it for today?" he asked.

"Yesterday I needed to get my hair done. Today, I need to go shopping. New clothes are definitely needed." His phone rang, and his whole mood changed once he saw who was calling. I figured it was his wife, because he left out of the room to go answer the phone. I rolled my eyes at the thought of her. At first, I didn't even care that he had a wife, but now that I was starting to catch feelings for him, I wanted her out of the picture.

I wanted Anthony all to myself. He and his wife hadn't even been together that long. Her name was Symone, and she just turned thirty-one about two weeks ago. Yeah, I did my research and found out everything about her. They didn't have any kids together, and I was happy about that. I wanted to be the first person to give Anthony a child. He said that he was too old to be having kids but I thought otherwise.

Lately, every time we have sex, I've been poking holes in the condoms. He was too stupid to realize what I was doing too, and I loved it. I was hoping that I was pregnant now; I just needed to go to the store so I could buy me a pregnancy test.

Anthony came back into the room, and he didn't look too happy either. I already knew he was about to leave so he could go be with her. That's always how it happens.

"Symone is sick, I gotta go home and check on her." he told me. It took everything in me not to roll my eyes at him and cuss him out about leaving me for that bitch.

"I hope she feels better soon so that you can come back to me." I said. He walked over to the bed and kissed me on my forehead. Then, he handed me some money before turning to leave. I made sure he was gone before I got up and started putting on clothes. I was thinking of ways that I could make Symone leave him. I knew she was with him for his money. Yeah, at first that's the only reason I was dealing with him, but that was before I caught feelings for him.

Once I was dressed, I grabbed my car keys off of the dresser and the money that he had left for me, and I was out of the house. I was excited as hell to find out if I was pregnant or not. When I got in the car, I called Nia... this girl that I met when I first got here. She wasn't really the type of people that I would normally hang out with, but she was the only friend that I had right now; we hung out almost every day.

"Hello?" she answered sounding like she was sleep.

"Hey bitch, what are you doing?"

"Well, I was sleep until you called. Why? What's up?"

"I'm about to come pick you up so get dressed." I hung up the phone before she could protest. Most of the time, she never feels like going anywhere with me, so she tries to come up with lame ass excuses as to why she can't go anywhere. She was coming with me whether she liked it or not, and I honestly didn't care how she felt though.

I met Nia when I went to the mall to pick up some new clothes, and we were both trying to buy the same shoes from Footlocker; they only had one pair left, and I had it in my mind that I was going to get those shoes, even if I had to beat her ass for them. I was prepared to fight, but to my surprise, she told me that I could have them. That's when I realized that she was a pushover, and she would be a great friend to have.

About fifteen minutes later, I pulled up to Nia's house, and I texted her to let her know that I was outside. It took about five minutes, but she finally emerged from her house, and I had to stop myself from laughing. She was wearing a light pink sweatsuit that said Baby Phat. What year was it? And she was still wearing Baby Phat like the shit was in. I shook my head as she got into the car.

"Where are you taking me?" she asked.

"I'm going to get a pregnancy test, then we're going to Red Lobster." I was starving. I wanted to go out to eat with Anthony but his stupid ass wife called.

"A pregnancy test? For what?"

"Because I think I'm pregnant. Duh. Why else would I be going to get one?" I said and rolled my eyes. I didn't know why she was acting so damn dumb.

"You're pregnant by that man who's married?" she asked.

"I might be. I'm not sure yet."

"If you are, are you going to keep it?" I looked at her then back at the road because I didn't want to crash.

"Of course I'm going to keep it. Why wouldn't I?" I asked feeling myself getting aggravated with this conversation.

"Because he's married, Londyn. I don't care what he says. He isn't leaving his wife so that he can be with you. You're just something to do when there's nothing to do. Why can't you see that? Why do you think he's always leaving you so that he can be with her? Because he loves her, and he

195

doesn't plan on leaving her anytime soon." I was wishing Nia would just shut up. She always thinks she knows everything when she didn't.

Anthony was going to leave his wife for me. His feelings were just as strong as mine were. Yeah, he never said anything about leaving his wife for me, but I knew that he wanted to, and if he took too long, I would help speed up the process. I had no problem getting rid of Symone. This time, I would actually have to kill her and not kidnap her.

I didn't say anything else to Nia because we had pulled up to Walgreens. I would just prove her wrong since she thought she knew some shit. I couldn't stand her sometimes. I got out of the car and she was right behind me as we walked into the store. I picked up the most expensive pregnancy test and then I went to go buy it. I couldn't stop smiling as the lady at the cash register rung me up. Nia stood beside me shaking her head.

"You can stop hating, Nia. One day you will find a man who's willing to give you the world too." I told her. She looked at me and laughed.

"Girl bye, I don't need a man to give me shit. I can spoil myself. I've done it before and I don't have a problem doing it now. I bet your little married boyfriend is going to tell you to get rid of it anyway." she laughed again. I wanted to hit her in her mouth, but instead, I just got my things and walked out of the store. I need to find new friends and soon. I don't know how much longer I was going to be able to put up with

Nia. She's always putting me down, and she's so negative. I didn't need that in my life. Especially not right now.

When we got back to my house, I basically ran into the bathroom so that I could pee on these tests. I didn't even invite Nia in the bathroom with me because I knew she would have something negative to say. I sat down on the sink waiting for these three minutes to hurry up. I felt like it took three years instead of three minutes, and I was so happy when it was time to see the results.

I picked up the two pregnancy tests and I was happy with what I saw. Two positive signs. I started jumping up and down, then I ran out of the bathroom. Nia was sitting in the living room watching Maury on T.V., then she looked up at me.

"Well, what did they say?" she asked not sounding too interested.

"I'm going to be a mommy." I said smiling hard as hell. She just shook her head at me and turned her attention back to the T.V. Shit, fuck her. I wasn't about to let her ruin my happiness. I was going to be a mother with the man that I loved. All I had to do was make sure that he left Symone, and if he didn't want to do it willingly, I had no problems doing it for him. We were going to be together and we were going to be a family, and I couldn't wait either.

Chapter Twenty-One

Jaxon

I really enjoyed spending time with Lena, but I could tell she was still stuck on her ex. She even said the bitch nigga's name in her sleep. I never brought it up to her because I knew she couldn't control what she said in her sleep, but still bothered me though. I wanted something with Lena, but I knew I wasn't going to get it while she was still in love with another nigga.

Lena was everything that I wanted in a female. She was smart, beautiful, and she had a good head on her shoulders. I could definitely see myself settling down with her and giving her my kids, but that just couldn't happen. I was in love with someone else too. That's why I wasn't really trippin' off of Lena.

I tried my hardest to move on and get her out of my system, but for some reason, I couldn't. All the shit that this girl had done to me, but I still wanted her. Even after five years. I lost five years of my life because of her. She set me up because she thought that I was cheating, and she didn't even call or write me while I was locked up. She basically just left me for dead, but none of that shit mattered to me anymore.

I guess Carla was my soul mate because if it had been any other female that did this to me, I would've been bodied them. I just couldn't bring myself to do it with Carla though. I couldn't kill her and I couldn't get anyone else to kill her for me. Just the thought of her dying fucked with me, and I didn't like that shit at all.

She was still calling and texting me, and I was trying not to answer to her, because I was always with Lena now, but the other night while Lena was at that pool party with Alani, she came to my club. I guess she was tired of me ignoring her, so she popped up on me. I wasn't expecting for her to show up looking as good as she did, though.

She was wearing an all-black dress that hugged her body and showed all of her curves. Her breasts looked like they had gotten a lot bigger than from when we were together five years ago. They were about to pop right out of her dress. I didn't even have to look at her ass to know that it was looking good too. She even had her curly hair straightened and flowing down her back. I had to keep looking away from her to get rid of the dirty thoughts that were invading my mind.

She wasn't having that though. While I was trying to explain to her why I couldn't be with her ever again because I couldn't trust her, she dropped to her knees and made my dick touch the back of her throat. Now who could focus on anything that was being said when a beautiful woman like Carla was trying to suck you dry? So what did I do? I let her do her thing. Then once she was finished, we fucked right there on the desk in my office.

After that night, all of my feelings that I had for her came rushing back. She was all that I was thinking about now. We were texting all day, every day, and talking on the phone when Lena wasn't around. I wasn't really cheating on Lena because we weren't in a relationship, right? She couldn't be mad at me. It wasn't like I was fucking the both of them at the same time or in the same day. I wasn't even having sex with Lena anymore, and I could tell that it was a problem for her too.

"So, who is she?" Lena asked once I got out of the shower. I wasn't expecting for this conversation to happen so soon.

"What are you talking about, Lena?" I asked playing dumb.

"Who is the new bitch that you met?"

"Why do you think I've met someone else?" She looked at me and chuckled.

"Nigga, stop trying to play me like I'm stupid. You text all day and smile at your phone, you're gone more than usual, and you stopped having sex with me, so who is she?" I didn't think she would notice all of this. Women really do pay attention to detail.

"Carla." I finally said. Since I was caught, there was no need to lie about it. She didn't say anything else to me. She just shook her head and got up off of the bed. Then, she went to the closet and started packing the things that she had over here.

"So you're not going to say anything?" I asked. I didn't like the silent treatment that she was giving me. I expected her to cuss me out or even try to fight me, but she didn't.

"What is there to say, Jax? It's obvious that I'll never be good enough for anyone so there's no need to even be mad or cause a scene about it. I don't know why you would want to be with the same chick that set you up and made you miss out on five years of your life, but who am I to judge?" she said making me feel bad as hell.

"Lena, we aren't even in a relationship." I reminded her. She stopped packing and looked up at me. I could see the tears threatening to fall and it made me feel even worse.

"Yeah, I know we weren't. But you know, I was hoping that maybe we could at least try. I was hoping that you would be different from my last relationship being that you knew what went on between us. I was hoping that if this isn't what you wanted then you could've at least let me know and not keep leading me on, but I guess that's all my fault for thinking you were different." She continued to pack her things, and I didn't say anything back to her. I couldn't find anything to say. I wanted to apologize but I didn't want to feel like an even bigger asshole, so I just watched her in silence as she got her things together.

"Tell Alani to call me when she wakes up." she said before leaving out of the room.

"Where are you going?" I asked.

"That doesn't matter to you anymore." She left out of the room and just left me standing there looking stupid. Maybe I should've tried to see where Lena and I could've went, but I felt like that would've been pointless because the heart wants what the heart wants and mine wanted Carla. I guess it was a little fucked up how everything happened, but hopefully down the line me and her could be friends again.

As soon as I laid down in my bed, my phone started ringing. I looked at the screen and saw that it was a text message from Carla.

Carla: I miss u. come see me.

I read it and sat my phone back down on the dresser. I wasn't in the mood to be dealing with anyone right now. I was tired as hell, so I just decided that I would see what was up with Carla tomorrow. She would probably be mad that I didn't reply to her message, but right now, I could care less. I closed my eyes and drifted off to sleep.

The next morning, I woke up to the smell of breakfast. I knew it was probably Alani cooking, so I got out of bed and made my way into the kitchen. I was surprised to see Carla standing at the stove and not Alani. Alani was sitting at the table with a bottle of Hennessy in her hands. She was looking like she was annoyed with Carla's presence.

"Carla, what are you doing here so early in the damn morning?" I asked.

"Well, you didn't text me back last night, so I just came over here because I remembered how much you loved waking up to breakfast." she smiled at me. Alani rolled her eyes.

"He wakes up to breakfast every morning. Lena was a great cook for my brother." Alani said being petty.

"Who is Lena?" Carla asked looking at me.

"Lena is my best friend that just moved out yesterday. I'm sure you saw her at my birthday party a couple of months ago." Alani said and smiled. I didn't even say anything. I just went into the refrigerator and got out some orange juice.

"You had that bitch living here?" Carla asked clearly bothered by what Alani had just told her.

"Don't be calling her a bitch. She doesn't disrespect you so don't disrespect her." I said.

"Wow Jax, you must really have feelings for this girl." Carla looked defeated. I did though. I had feelings for Lena, and I didn't realize how strong they were until she left. I was starting to feel like I made a mistake by fucking with Carla again. What if she did the same shit to me again? But what if it was worse and I got more than five years?

"You don't have to worry about Lena, Carla. She left him. Now you can have him all to yourself but don't think for a second that I like your ass. I could never fuck with a grimy bitch like you. And if you do some shit like that to my brother again, bitch, I will kill you." Alani said standing up. It scared me a little bit because I never saw Alani so serious about something. I didn't expect for her to like Carla so soon though. I would have to give it time just like I had to give it time. Alani walked out of the kitchen before Carla could even say anything.

She looked scared as hell. Carla had never been the fighting type. That's another reason why I felt like she set me up. Because she couldn't fight the chick she claimed I was cheating with. She even got her ass beat at Alani's party by Harlem. That's something that I didn't like about her though. She was always running her mouth and couldn't back it up. That was on her though.

"How long do you think Alani is going to hate me?" she asked sitting down at the table. I sat down in front of her.

"Who knows? You did do some fucked up shit to me. I missed out on five years of my only sister's life because of you. Then on top of all that, her and your brother are going through some shit. She might not ever like you again." I honestly said.

"Well, I'm not going to just sit back and let her disrespect me, Jaxon." I couldn't help but laugh at her.

"What's going to happen if she keeps disrespecting you? You gonna beat her ass? You know damn well you can't fight so that's an ass whoopin' waiting to happen."

"So you're just going to let her keep disrespecting me? I wouldn't do that if Los was constantly disrespecting you."

"I'm a grown ass man, and I can handle myself, for one. Two, Alani doesn't like you at all. So no, I'm not going to say anything about her disrespecting you. If you wouldn't have set me up to begin with we wouldn't be going through none of this." Carla didn't say anything else. She just sat there stuck in her thoughts. I guess she was finally realizing that it was going to take a while before we could get back to what we used to be, but that was all her fault though.

Alani walked back into the kitchen wearing a short ass dress that you would see a video chick wearing in one of those music videos.

"Where the hell are you going?" I asked not feeling her outfit at all.

"I'm going to a friend's house."

"Not dressed like that you're not." She rolled her eyes at me.

"Boy bye. I'm grown as hell and you are not my daddy. I can wear whatever I want."

"Who's your friend anyway? Lena?"

"Don't be trying to worry about Lena now, nigga. And his name is Juice. That's where I'm going. I'll be back later. Or not. Depends on how I'm feeling later." She came and kissed me on my cheek then made her way to the door.

"Bye Alani." Carla called out to her before she left.

"Girl, shut the fuck up." Alani spat then left out of the door. I tried my hardest not to laugh but I couldn't help it. Alani was so rude and she didn't care at all. Carla looked like she was on the verge of tears.

"It's not funny! I can't believe you're laughing at this. She's never going to like me." she pouted.

"You'll be okay. You're not fuckin' her anyway. Her opinion of you shouldn't matter."

"Well, if you could keep her away from me…" I cut her off before she could even finish her statement.

"Nah. She lives here now. I'm not about to tell her that she can't be here because you feel some type of way that she doesn't like you. Get the fuck over that shit. Start acting like a grown woman." She rolled her eyes and didn't say anything else, so I decided to go back upstairs so that I could find me something to wear. Of course Carla followed me.

"So, was that Lena girl sleeping in this bed with you?" she asked sitting on the bed.

"She was. Every night."

"And you expect for me to be okay with this? I'm not sleeping in the bed that you were fucking another bitch in!" *Here she goes with all of this dramatic shit.* I was starting to wish she wouldn't have brought her ass over here. I can't even get dressed in peace.

"We're not together." I said.

"Okay, but we're working on it, right? Until you get a new bed, I'm not having sex with you at all." she said folding her arms across her chest. I looked at her and realized how good she was looking in a tan jumpsuit that had her breasts spilling out of the top. She had her hair up in a tight bun on the top of her head and she had light make up on. She didn't need that at all but she wore it anyway.

"You're not having sex with me until when?" I asked walking closer to her.

"Until you buy a new bed." She was so serious, and it was cute. I laughed at her and pushed her back on the bed.

"Jaxon, stop." she said trying to fight me off of her but she wasn't strong enough at all. I started kissing her on her neck as her cries for me to stop slowly turned into moans. I removed her jumpsuit and she wasn't wearing anything underneath it. I took one of her breasts into my mouth and swirled my tongue around the nipple.

"Jax… Stop." she weakly said. She knew she didn't want me to stop. I reached my hand down so that I could play with her clit, and she was already soaking wet. I chuckled to myself as I stood up and dropped my boxers. Spreading her legs, I plunged into her forcefully, and she yelled out. She was screaming at the top of her lungs like I was killing her or some shit.

"Jaxonnn! Don't… Stoppp!" she yelled. I didn't even care that I had went inside of her raw. She was feeling too damn good for me to pull out. I felt myself about to cum, and I didn't want that to happen yet. I tried to pull out of her to regain my composure, but she started squeezing her pussy around my dick.

"Ohh, I'm cumming!" she moaned. I wasn't too far behind her either. I couldn't pull out even if I wanted to, so I hope she was on some form of birth control.

"I hate you." she said as I collapsed on top of her. I kissed her on her cheek.

"Nah, you love a nigga."

"Did you pull out?" That right there let me know that she wasn't on any type of birth control. *Shit.*

"Nah, I thought you were on birth control." I rolled off of her and sat up in bed.

"Why would you think that? I never said anything like that!" she yelled.

"Well, you knew what I was about to do. You saw that I didn't have a condom on. You could've said something." She was making a big deal out of this. If she got pregnant, I was going to be just fine with it. I mean, she was the girl that I planned on spending the rest of my life with.

"I'm going to get a plan B pill." she said making me want to punch the shit out of her.

"If you do that, don't bother hitting me up no more." I was dead ass serious about that too. Why the hell is she making such a big deal out of this?

"Are you serious? I'm not ready to have a baby, Jaxon."

"Okay, and I am. So if you go and get that bullshit ass pill, you don't have to worry about us getting back to how we used to be. I'll just find me a girl that's willing to have my kids. And you know there's plenty of them." Carla didn't say anything else. She just sat there looking stupid. I was serious though. She was trying to kill my baby before there was even a baby, and I wasn't fucking with that shit at all. It was obvious that Carla had a lot of growing up to do. I could already tell that it was going to take us a while to get back to how we used to be. I just hoped all of this would be worth it.

Chapter Twenty-Two

Lena

I felt like I couldn't catch a break. It seems like every nigga that I start messing with all do the same thing. Yeah, I know that Jaxon and I weren't in a relationship, but for him to tell me that he was fucking with Carla again was a slap to the face. I was starting to develop feelings for him and this is what he does. He didn't even have the decency to let me know that he wasn't feeling me anymore.

So here I was, stripping again to make my money. I was so over dealing with these ain't shit niggas. I'm convinced that they're all going to do the same thing to me in the end which is just play with my emotions. I knew I should've just left him alone. When he called me that night, that should've been the only conversation that we had, and now I felt like a complete fool.

I had gotten me another apartment, so I when I left from Jaxon's house, I went to go set up everything in there. I already had furniture from when I put everything in storage when I was about to leave for Jacksonville. After I put all of my clothes away, I sat down on the bed and turned on the T.V. I was really in my feelings right now, and I needed to get me a drink. I didn't have anything here to drink, so I decided to just go to the bar and get me something.

I didn't care about dressing up and getting cute or anything like that. I just put on some denim jeans and a black t-shirt. It was night time, and I wasn't going to the bar so that I could find me another boyfriend. I was trying to stay away from men for a long time. It seemed like none of the ones that I messed with were serious. Maybe it just wasn't meant for me to be in a relationship. I was going to be single until further notice.

When I got inside of the bar, I ordered three shots of Hennessy. I needed something strong, and I knew brown liquor would do it for me. After I was finished with the first three shots, I ordered three more, and this shit was strong as hell. I didn't know how Alani drank this for breakfast every morning.

"Don't you think you need to slow down?" I heard a familiar voice say. I didn't even have to turn around to know who the voice belonged to. He sat down on the stool beside me and smiled, and I rolled my eyes hard as hell at him.

"Don't you need to be somewhere fucking my cousin?" I spat. I ordered three more shots. Why did this nigga have to be here? I came here to get some peace and of course he shows up. Stupid ass nigga.

"I don't fuck with Draya like that no more." he said like I was supposed to believe him. I ignored him and continued to down my shots. "Lena, will you just hear me out?" he asked. I looked at him and quickly looked away. He was looking too damn good for me to hear anything he had to say. I knew how this would end. I would end up riding his dick until the sun came up, and I didn't have time for that. I was trying to get over Ali, and him being at the bar with me right now was making it even harder.

"Look, when I first met Draya, I didn't know that she was your cousin. You had left without telling anyone where you went and I was feeling fucked up about it. I went to go get me some liquor and she was the cashier. She was flirting with me and shit, so I told her to come chill with me at the room that I had. Long story short, I ended up taking her virginity and from there we became fuck buddies. That bitch was never my girlfriend. The only girl that I want is you. She was just something to do to pass the time until you came back to me." he said. I didn't know what to say. I didn't know he took her virginity either. Now the bitch wasn't ever going to leave him alone.

I shook my head and looked at him. I guess part of it was my fault because I had left, but he was the reason I left.

"I left because you don't know how to keep your dick in your pants." I finally said after just looking at him.

"I know, I fucked up. I don't even know why I did it. I was drunk and she was throwing it at me. I wish I wouldn't have done it at all."

"Yeah, I bet you do. It's too late now. You really fucked up when you got with my cousin. Then once you found out that she was my cousin, you were still fucking with her. Taking her shopping and shit. Nigga, you ain't sorry.

213

You're only sorry that you got caught." I was drunk now. The shots really had me feeling myself.

"It wasn't even like that, Lena." he tried to explain.

"Then what was it like? You can't keep your dick in your pants. I wish I would've known that before I started dealing with you." Ali looked hurt by my words but I didn't care. I wanted him to be hurt. I wanted him to know how it felt to get your heart ripped out by someone you love. I stood up off of the stool and I felt myself getting dizzy; I had had too much to drink. I didn't even plan on drinking that much, but Ali came and I felt like I needed way more to drink than I actually did.

"Lena?" I heard Ali say before I fell to the ground and everything went black.

I woke up the next morning in a bed that didn't belong to me. The room wasn't familiar to me at all either. It had to belong to someone that had money though. I could tell. The only thing I remembered from last night was going to the bar and Ali showing up. Everything else was really a blur.

"Good morning beautiful." Ali said coming into the room. This nigga. He wasn't wearing anything but his boxers and he had a tray of food in his hands. Smelling the food made me realize how much I missed his cooking. He sat the tray in front of me then he went to sit on the other side of the bed.

"How are you feeling?" he asked. I rolled my eyes at him. We were not friends, and we were not on good terms at all, so I don't even know why he brought me back here.

"Fine." I said dryly.

"You sure? You hit your head pretty hard last night when you fell." Now that he said something, my head was throbbing.

"I'm good." I said eating the pancakes that were on my plate. He also had some pain pills and orange juice on the tray too. He was making it really hard for me to be upset with him.

"Whose house are we in?" I asked once I finished eating and took the pills.

"Mine."

"Yours? When did you move?" I knew he had Draya living in his other house with him. I wonder if she was still there.

"The other day. I wanted to buy us a new house so we could start over." I looked at him and he was serious. I don't think I was ready to forgive him just yet. He's done too much just for me to let him back in, and I didn't want him to think that it was okay for him to cheat on me because he thinks I'm just going to take him back.

"Well, you can tell Draya that y'all two have a nice new house together so she can move out of the other one." I said.

"I already told you that I wasn't fucking with Draya anymore. I want you and only you. She never even lived with me. I would just let her spend the night and shit. But that's the past. I'm turning over a new leaf so that I can be with the one woman I'm actually in love with."

"It's going to take way more than just you moving me into your new house." I said. He smiled at me like I had just told him that I was going to marry him or something.

"I know, but it's a start." The doorbell rang and he left the room to go answer it. I was just sitting on the bed wondering who the hell was at the door. He just moved here, so who knew where he lived already?

A few moments later, Ali came back into the room and started putting on clothes. This nigga was about to leave me here? Oh, I think not.

"Where are you going?" I asked with an attitude.

"I'm not going anywhere. I got a meeting with Los. I'll just be downstairs." he said kissing me on my forehead. I wanted to leave. I wonder what he did with my car since he was the one who brought me home last night. I hope they didn't tow it away or anything. Being that it was just Los downstairs, I decided to go down there and ask Ali about my car, and when the hell he was taking me home. I was not trying to be here all day.

Walking down the stairs, I was taken aback by the beauty of the house. This house looked so much better than the last one, and I could really get used to living here with him. I just didn't know how long it would be before I was comfortable enough to move in with him again. I have to make sure he and I are on the same page before we cross that line again.

Los was sitting on the couch looking like he hadn't had any good sleep in days. Then, on top of that, he had some bitch with him. She was really comfortable sitting on his lap, too. It must've been Tammy's mom; she was so wrong for fucking her daughter's baby daddy.

"What's up, Lena?" I heard a familiar voice say. I turned around to see Legend coming out of the kitchen with a beer in his hand. What the hell was he doing here in Ali's house? How the hell did they know each other?

"Hey, what are you doing here?"

"I work for Ali now. I didn't know that was your nigga." he said, going to sit down on the couch.

"Yeah... I guess." was all I said.

"How's Alani doing?" he asked. My eyes shot right to Los. He was burning a hole through Legend now. Damn. Legend doesn't even know what he has gotten himself into.

"She's good."

"How the fuck you know Alani?" Los asked.

"I met her when she was living in Jacksonville. Shawty had an ass on her." I was staring at Legend so hard wishing he would just shut up.

"What nigga?" Los said pushing the chick off of his lap and standing up. Legend didn't know about Los and Alani. Otherwise, he probably wouldn't have said anything. Especially now since he was working for them.

"Los, he didn't know about y'all two. Chill out." I said standing in front of Los. Los grilled the fuck out of Legend before he sat back down.

"I better not hear her name come out of your mouth ever again, my nigga." Los told him. I could tell that the bitch he was with wasn't too happy about how he had just reacted over Alani. Shit, I wasn't happy either because not once had he tried to call her or check up on her. He really wasn't shit.

Ali came back into the living room finally. He had missed everything that had just happened. I looked over at Legend, and it seemed like he had a look of satisfaction on his face. Like he wanted to make Los mad on purpose. Maybe I was just trippin'.

"Lena, what you doing?" Ali asked.

"Wondering when you're going to take me home."

"Take yo' ass back upstairs. We'll talk about that when I'm finished with this meeting." I rolled my eyes at him and made my way back up the stairs. When I got back up there, I saw that my phone was ringing. It was Alani, so I rushed to answer it.

"Hello?" I said.

"Damn, bitch. What the hell you doing? I called your ass like ten times." she said. She didn't sound drunk today and I was happy about that. Maybe she was going to cut back on the drinking.

"My bad, I was downstairs with Ali. What's up though?"

"What the hell you doing with Ali?" she asked; I had forgotten that I didn't call and tell her about my night.

"Oh, well I went to the bar last night after I left your brother's house and I ran into Ali. Long story short, I got too drunk and passed out so he took me home. Bitch, he bought a new damn house for us. This shit is huge." I said.

"So are y'all back together?"

"No, not at all. I'm not even moving in with him yet. I'm not ready for all that. I don't even know if he's ready for all of this. I guess this is just a trial run."

"Well as long as you're happy, I'm happy. But anyways, tell me why that Carla bitch comes to the house this morning cooking breakfast and shit like she lives there. Seeing her stupid ass face made me want to punch her in it so damn bad." Of course Carla was at the house. This shit didn't surprise me at all.

"Fuck that bitch." I spat. I didn't want to sound jealous, but I was. Yeah, I was still very much in love with Ali but I still had feelings for Jaxon too.

"I feel like I'm going to have to beat her ass. I had to leave. Being in her presence was fucking with me. I don't think I'm going to be staying there with him anymore."

"Where are you going to live then?"

"With a friend." She didn't want me to know who she was moving in with, but I felt like I already knew.

"A friend? What's his name?" I asked.

"What makes you think it's a guy? It could be a girl." I laughed at her silly ass.

"Girl bye, you don't like females. So who's the nigga that you're staying with?"

"Juice." she quietly said, but I heard it anyway. I knew it anyway. She knew she was feeling him more than she wanted to admit, but I didn't understand why she was playing though.

"Oh, I knew that. Tell him I said hey." I giggled.

"Shut up bitch, you didn't know shit. But I'm about to go swimming in his big ass pool. I'll call you later." she said then ended the call before I could even protest. As soon as we go off of the phone, a text message came through.

Jaxon: What's good? I miss u

I looked at the text message and laughed. What the hell was wrong with these niggas? They act like they can just hurt you and then send a text message that would make everything so much better. I didn't even bother responding back to him. He should be happy with that grimy bitch that set him up. I can bet money that she's going to do some fucked up shit to him again, but that's not my problem anymore. I needed to worry about my own relationship. I just hoped that Ali knew how to act this time because if he fucks up again, then I'm gone for good.

Chapter Twenty-Three

Legend

I knew exactly what I was doing when I brought up Alani's name. I knew it would make him mad, but I don't know why. From what I'm hearing, they aren't even together anymore and she's been chillin' with that nigga Juice. I didn't care that Los got all into his bitch ass feelings when I said her name. I wanted him to.

See, I was working for Ali and Los, and I couldn't stand these two niggas for shit. They thought they were untouchable but they weren't. I planned on getting rid of the both of them and taking over. They killed my brother, Josh, so they had to pay for it. I knew they had killed him, because Josh told me that he had gotten himself into some shit and had to have the government protect him. Obviously, that shit didn't work because my brother still ended up dead, and I knew exactly who was behind it.

I knew who Alani and Lena were back when we were all still in Jacksonville. I had been planning on moving to Miami to get at these niggas. I wondered how Los was going to react when he found out that I was fucking his bitch back in Jacksonville, and I planned on telling him right before I killed his stupid ass.

"Legend, you're not even listening to me!" Leslie yelled. I was starting to get tired of her. All she did was nag and complain. Ever since she caught me fucking Alani, she thinks I'm always with another bitch. I mean, most of the time I was, but so what? I'm getting more money now than I was ever getting in Jacksonville. It's not my fault the bitches flock.

"What are you complaining about now?" I asked already annoyed with this conversation.

"I asked you if you liked my hair." Looking at her hair, I knew exactly who she got the idea from. Her hair was shoulder length and it was red. She was trying her hardest to be like Alani, but it wasn't working. She could never be Alani. No matter how hard she tried.

"It's alright." I said scrolling through my phone looking for Alani's Instagram page. I went on her page every day just to see her beautiful face. I didn't know what it was about her, but she was all I had been thinking about lately. I needed her in my life. I hadn't seen her at all since I got to Miami, and I wasn't too happy about that.

"What do you mean it's alright? You don't like it?"

"I like it better on Alani. And hers is actually her real hair because she has hair unlike you." Leslie looked at me like she wanted to cry. Then she started laughing.

"So because I got my hair like this, I'm trying to be like Alani? Don't nobody give a fuck about that bitch. You're always bringing her name up. Why don't you go be with that bitch then?"

"Believe me, if I could I would. I wouldn't be here with your dry pussy ass." Leslie came over and slapped the shit out of me. I wasn't expecting for her to do that at all. I wasn't the type of nigga to put my hands on a female though, so I bit the insides of my cheek to stop myself from hitting her back.

"Fuck you nigga! You ain't shit! Los didn't think that my pussy was dry!" she yelled with tears streaming down her face. I just laughed at her because she thought I gave a fuck. I didn't give a fuck about this relationship anymore. After I got a taste of Alani, I realized that Leslie wasn't woman enough for me. She only came to Miami with me to make sure I wasn't doing anything I wasn't supposed to be doing, but I was because I didn't give a fuck about her or her feelings.

"Go live with that nigga then. Get your shit and get the fuck out." I calmly said. She didn't like that I said that at all.

"Are you serious?" she asked on the verge of tears.

"As a heart attack. He won't be alive too much longer anyway." I laughed to myself.

"What? You're going to kill him?"

"Get the fuck out my face, Leslie. You're being annoying as hell right now." I said while still looking through Alani's pictures. I needed to see her and hear her voice. I didn't know if she would be up for that or not. My phone rang while I was liking all of Alani's pictures.

"Hello?" I said a little aggravated because whoever was calling me was interrupting me while I was trying to look at Alani.

"What's good Legend? Let's meet up somewhere." Los said into the phone.

"Aight, where?"

"The trap house on the west." he said and ended the call. This right here is why I didn't like him. He didn't have to hang up on me. His cockiness was going to get him killed, and I couldn't wait to put two bullets in his skull. I was smiling just thinking about it.

"Who was that? Your other bitch?" Leslie asked. I forgot she was still standing there.

"Don't worry about it. I'll be back later though." I said getting up off of the couch and walking to my car. I wonder what this nigga wanted to meet about. I hope he wasn't on no bullshit though. I wasn't in the mood for it.

As I was backing out of the driveway, I realized I didn't have the strap on me. I didn't want to turn around and go back in the house, so I just said fuck it and kept it moving. I probably wouldn't need it anyway. He was probably just going to discuss business with me anyway. I just hoped it didn't take too long, because I was still trying to figure out how I was going to see Alani.

When I got to the trap house, Los was standing outside talking on the phone. As soon as he saw me, he ended the call and motioned for me to follow him into the house. I followed behind him and watched as he took a seat at the table. It was a small table with only two chairs at it. There were other niggas in the house, but they weren't paying any attention to us.

"Now, if there's one thing I don't like, it's a liar. That will get you bodied real quick. So I'm gonna ask you this once. What did you and Alani have going on?" he asked lighting a blunt. I didn't expect for him to ask me about this. I thought he made me come here for business. Not to talk about a bitch he wasn't even with anymore.

"Nothing." I lied. He looked at me and chuckled.

"What did I just say?" he asked putting his pistol on the table. My heart rate sped up. I knew I should've turned around and got my gun from out of the house.

"I mean, she was cool to chill with." I said fumbling with my words. I wasn't trying to die today. I had things in life that I wanted to do. I felt like if I told him that I was fucking Alani, he would still kill my ass.

"Damn, I thought you had more balls than that." Los said laughing and removing the safety off of his gun. *Shit.*

"I know y'all fucked around, nigga. I'm not stupid. I could see it all over your stupid ass face yesterday when you brought her name up. I could've killed you right then and there, but I didn't. I didn't want to disrespect my cousin's house like that. But right now, I don't give a fuck. I could put two in your head and not lose an ounce of sleep over it." He said looking me dead in my eyes,

"Yeah, I fucked her but she told me she was single." I blurted out. Los laughed at me.

"So you trying to call my girl a hoe now?"

"What? No. I'm just wondering why you're mad that your bitch was on me. You should be mad at her. Not me." Before I realized what I had said, Los was out of his seat and was pistol whipping my ass. I wasn't even expecting this. I tried to fight back but this nigga was like the energizer bunny. I don't think I landed any of my punches.

I felt my mouth fill up with my blood and I felt the bones in my nose crack. This nigga wasn't letting up at all. I was starting to get mad because there were at least five other niggas that were in this house and they weren't even trying to pull this nigga off of me. I had never got my ass beat like this. Usually, niggas are the ones that're afraid of me, but with Los, it was a different story.

With every hit, my hatred for him grew even more. I wish I could kill this nigga right now. I was slowly starting to drift in and out of consciousness, and before I knew it, everything went black.

I woke up on the couch in the same trap house with Los standing over me. My body felt like it had been hit by a ton of bricks. My head was pounding and my face felt like it was on fire. I looked up at Los who was wearing a smile on his face. Ali was standing beside him.

"How you feeling little nigga?" Ali asked. I couldn't stand his ass either.

"Nah, fuck all that. I better not see you comment on any of Alani's pictures anymore. Don't like them shits either. If I catch you trying to talk to her, I'm killing your ass. If I even think you're thinking about her, I'm killing your ass. We clear?" Los asked me. I just nodded my head. This nigga had me feeling like a complete bitch. It was all good though. His time was coming soon. He could think he was invincible all he wanted. He wouldn't think that when I was killing his ass. His days were numbered. He wouldn't even be expecting the shit either and I couldn't wait.

Chapter Twenty-Four

Los

Mad was an understatement. Knowing that Alani fucked with this bitch ass nigga made me want to put my hands on her. Beating Legend's ass made me feel good as fuck, though, and I was glad that I had done it too.

"Bruh, you good?" Ali asked as he drove me home. I was digging in my pockets looking for a pill but my pockets were empty. *Shit.* I thought to myself as I remembered I had taken the last two pills before I called Legend to meet up.

"You got any bars on you?" I asked him. He looked at me then quickly back at the road.

"Nigga, you're out already? That bag was big as hell." he said. I wasn't in the mood to hear him lecturing me and shit. It was a yes or no question. Simple.

"Do you have any or not nigga?" I knew he had some on him. He always did because he was selling them shits. He sighed then pointed to the glove compartment. I opened it, and it was three bags of pills. I took one bag and opened it.

"Nigga, hell nah. Wait till you get out of my car before you start poppin' them shits. I'm not supporting your habit so make this the last time you ask me for any of them pills." he said. I thought he was joking at first, but when I looked at him, I saw that he was dead ass serious. I wanted to be mad at him, but I couldn't. This was his car, and I had to respect that. I held the bag in my hand as I impatiently waited for him to take me home.

"Just drop me off at Janelle's crib." I said, because I couldn't wait any longer. I knew I was acting like a fiend, but I didn't care right now. I needed these pills, and I needed them right now. Ali didn't say anything to me as he pulled up to Janelle's house.

"Thanks bruh." I said getting out of the car.

"You need to take care of that problem and soon before you take it too far." Ali said.

"I already told you that I was good. I don't even have a problem." He nodded his head, and I shut his door. He drove off as I made my way to Janelle's front door.

"Hey, bae. I didn't expect for you to be here so early." Janelle said hugging me. I gently pushed her off of me and went into the kitchen so that I could pop these pills. I pulled out a bottle of water from the fridge and then I looked at the bag of pills that I had.

"Babe, you popped two of those two hours ago. Now you're about to take some more?" Janelle said coming into the kitchen.

"Mind yo' business man." I said not even turning around to look at her. She was acting like I was snorting cocaine up my nose or some shit. I stopped what I was doing because I had just got an idea. If I take these as a powder, it would be a lot stronger. I would be high as hell.

I went into her kitchen drawer and got two spoons out. Putting two of the pills on the counter, I crushed them up until they were a fine powder.

"Los, what are you doing?" Janelle asked. I ignored her and continued with what I was doing. Once I was satisfied with the powder, I scooped it into the spoon and then I poured it into my mouth. It was nasty as hell, but I didn't give not one fuck. I took the water bottle and drank the whole thing before walking back into the living and sitting down on the couch.

Five minutes had past, and I could feel the pills starting to take effect. I felt good as hell sitting on the couch. I could hear my son crying, and I could hear Janelle saying shit to me, but I couldn't move. I couldn't even make out what it was that Janelle was saying. I closed my eyes as I drifted off to sleep.

~~~~~~

I woke up on the floor in the living room of my house. *How the fuck did I get here?* The last thing I remembered was falling asleep on the couch at Janelle's house. I sat up and looked around. My mouth was dry as hell, and I needed something to drink bad. I stood all the way up and went into the kitchen. There were about four empty water bottles on the table and the peanut butter and jelly were out. I guess I had made myself a sandwich and didn't even remember it. I don't remember shit.

I got me a water bottle out of refrigerator then went to go sit down on the couch. I pulled my phone out of my pocket and went straight to Alani's Instagram page. I did this every day just to see her face. I missed the hell out of her. I wasn't acting like it, but I did miss her crazy ass. I was supposed to be getting myself together so that I could get her back, but I haven't done anything but gotten worse. I needed to talk to her.

I quickly got up off of the couch and grabbed my car keys. I was then out of the door and on my way to Jaxon's crib. I was pretty sure that that was where Alani was so I was just going to show up and let her know how sorry I was for hurting her and shit. The bag of pills were in the passenger seat, and it took everything in me not to pop a couple of them. I wanted to talk to Alani with a clear head, because there was no telling what I might've said if I was high off of pills.

I got to Jaxon's house and quickly got out of the car. I knocked on his door and waited for him to open it. I was surprised when Carla opened the door. *What the hell is she doing over here?*

"Carlos? Are you okay? You look terrible." she said.

"Fuck all that, where's Alani at?"

"She moved."

"Moved? What the fuck you mean she moved?" I yelled louder than I wanted to. Jaxon came to the door, and I could tell he was surprised to see me.

"What's up?" he asked.

"Where's Alani?" I asked. The face he made let me know that he didn't want me to know where Alani was. I didn't understand why though.

"She's good." was his response.

"Nigga, I didn't ask you all that! I asked you where she was."

"I heard you, my nigga. I'm letting you know that she's good. Don't come trying to worry about her now. You wasn't worried about her when she was crying herself to sleep for two weeks straight. You wasn't worried about her when she was drinking for breakfast, lunch, and dinner. When she left, she finally looked like her normal self. Leave her alone, bruh. You ain't no good for her." I wanted to punch this nigga in his shit, but it was my fault that Alani was sad; I didn't call to check up on her at all.

"I heard she moved in with some nigga." Carla said. I grilled the fuck out of her for saying some shit like that, but she was serious. I was ready to kill whoever that nigga was now. I didn't say anything else to them. I just walked away and got into my car. I dialed Alani's number, and it rang a couple of times before going to voicemail. She ignored my call. *Man, what the fuck.*

I was so mad that I was shaking. I picked up the bag of pills before putting my hand in there and pulling out a handful. I put every single last one of them in my mouth and drank the water that was rolling around on the floor.

"Carlos!" I heard Carla yell. She was coming towards my car.

"What?" I said opening the door.

"What's going on with you? Are you okay?" she asked.

"Yeah, I'm good." I was getting tired of telling people that I was good. I wish they would stop asking.

"Why won't you return any of mommy's phone calls then? She's really worried about you." I've been ignoring my mom, because I knew she would have a lot to say about my pill addiction. I wasn't trying to hear any of that shit right now. I kept telling myself that I would call her later, but later never came.

"Carlos? Did you hear me?" I heard Carla say, but I couldn't say anything back to her. I couldn't do anything. I could barely keep my eyes open. I felt myself fall out of the car and onto the hard concrete.

"Oh my goodness! Carlos!" I heard Carla yell before everything went black.

Chapter Twenty-Five

Alani

I sat in the waiting room of the hospital not really knowing how I should feel. I didn't know if I should leave or if I should stay. Should I really go back there and see the man that I was still so madly in love with, or should I just leave because he broke my heart? I knew I should've answered the phone when he called, but Juice was too busy feasting on my kitty, and I couldn't answer the phone if I wanted to.

Getting the call from Lena that Los had overdosed had me stuck. What the fuck did he overdose on? His life had really gotten that bad to the point that he had to start doing drugs? I rushed out of the house without even telling Juice where I was going. I was sure he wasn't going to be too happy about this later.

The lady at the desk had already told me what room Los was in, but I wasn't prepared to go back there yet. Lena was there sitting right beside me, because she knew that I wouldn't be able to do this on my own.

"I'm ready." I let her know after another five minutes had passed. We both stood up and made our way to the direction of the room that he was in. I felt my heart get heavier and heavier with every step I took. I didn't think I was ready, but it was too late to turn back now.

Walking into his room, I was glad to see that he was awake, but I wasn't happy to see that bitch in here with him. She was giving him a kiss on the lips when I walked in. Once again, this nigga had ripped my heart out.

"Janelle." Lena said, making them both look at us. Los looked terrible. His hair was everywhere, his face was sunken in, and he looked like he hadn't had a good sleep in about a month.

"What is she doing here? As I recall, you're not his woman anymore. I am." she said, holding her hand up and showing a ring. Carlos didn't say anything though. He just looked at me like he wanted to love all over me but he couldn't because his girlfriend was right there. Or should I say fiancé? I didn't say anything as I turned to leave the room. Lena was right behind me.

"Alani, I didn't know she was here. I wouldn't have told you to come here had I known she was here." Lena said. I still didn't say anything though. I just wanted to go home and lay under Juice. He had a way of making me feel better no matter what I was going through.

"Just take me home." I said. She nodded her head and started the car.

"Alani, I really am sorry." Lena kept apologizing, but it wasn't her fault at all. She shouldn't have felt bad. She was just being a good friend by taking me up there to see his no good ass. He sure did move on quickly, but I guess that wasn't my problem anymore. I needed to get him out of my system, and what better way to do that than by moving on to some new dick? I hadn't had sex with Juice because I felt like I was disrespecting Los, but all that had just went out of the window. I was going to be a porn star tonight. He wasn't even going to be expecting it.

Once Lena dropped me off, I went straight to the kitchen so that I could get me something to drink. I wanted to drink the whole bottle, but I had cut back on my drinking. I didn't want to become an alcoholic so I had to stop drinking as much as I did.

"You straight? You just left without letting a nigga know where you were going." Juice said coming into the kitchen. He was looking so good in his gray Nike joggers. He wasn't wearing a shirt, and his tattoos were on display making my mouth water. His dick print was on full display, too, so I sat my cup down on the table and walked over to him.

"You think the counter is high enough to fuck on it?" I asked. He looked at the counter, then back at me. Without a word, he picked me up and sat me on the counter. He removed my pants then put his lips on mine. He tasted like a mint. That's what he always smelled like and I loved it.

He ran his fingers across my clit making me moan into his mouth. Then, he dropped his pants and slid into me with ease.

"Shit." he whispered into my ear. I hadn't had dick in so long, I almost forgot what it felt. It hurt like hell though.

"Wait," I said but Juice wasn't listening. He had his eyes closed, and he was biting his bottom lip. He was in the zone, not even caring that I was in pain. A few moments later, it started to feel better.

"Juiceee," I moaned while throwing my hands around his neck.

"Shit girl." he grunted. I felt myself about to cum, but I didn't want to yet. I wanted to hold out until he was about to cum too.

"I'm gonna cumm!" I yelled. He spread my legs even wider and started going harder. This nigga was really showing me no mercy. I felt myself exploding all over him, and he quickly pulled out. He got himself together then slid back in. I closed my eyes trying not to scream at the top of my lungs because I hadn't experienced this feeling in a while.

"Ahh, fuckk!" he yelled and pulled out. He came all over the counter then looked at me.

"You made me do that nasty shit." he said

"Shut up nigga, you could've done it somewhere else." He helped me down from the counter, and we went upstairs to take a shower together. From there, we fucked in the shower, then once we got out, we fucked for the rest of the night until we passed out.

~~~~~~

It had been about a week since Los had overdosed, and I hadn't heard from him at all. I wasn't surprised or anything since he did have a fiancé that was taking care of him. I was really wishing that I would've never taken my ass up there to the hospital; it was pointless.

"I got company coming over. You should put some clothes on." Juice said to me. I wasn't wearing anything but some boy shorts and one of Juice's shirts.

"But I'm so comfortable. Why do they have to come over here anyway?" I pouted. I didn't feel like putting on clothes.

"Girl, stop being a baby and go put on some clothes. They want to meet you." he said. Who the fuck wanted to meet me? I hope it wasn't his family or anything because all Juice and I were doing was fucking. I didn't plan on having a relationship with him at all. I rolled my eyes and got up off of the couch so that I could go put on some pants.

I just threw on some leggings because I really didn't care about how I was looking right now. I put my hair up in a messy bun and put on one of my tank tops. I heard voices downstairs, so I made my way back down there.

"This is my girl, Alani." Juice said. Everyone on the couch turned to look at me, and right now I wished I was anywhere but here. I locked eyes with Carlos, and I swear, I could see the fire in them. He looked from me to Juice and started laughing.

"You fucking my bitch?" Los asked Juice. Juice had a confused look on his face. He didn't know what was going on at all.

"Nigga, fuck you talking about?" Juice asked. Los got off of the couch and made his way towards me. I noticed that he had his gun out as he was approaching me, and I was scared as hell, because I just knew he was about to kill me.

"Alani, you fucking this nigga?!" he yelled while aiming the gun at my head.

"Carlos, I…"

POW! POW! POW!

To Be Continued…

CPSIA information can be obtained
at www.ICGtesting.com
Printed in the USA
LVOW13s1312270318
571320LV00020B/583/P